BOSSY NIGHTS

LIV MORRIS

Copyright © 2018 Liv Morris
Editing by Word Nerd Editing
Proofreading by Proofing Style
Faye Howe and Tracey S.
Cover Design by RBA Design
Photograph by Scott Hoover
Cover Model Stuart Reardon

Welcome to Hammond Press

1

TESSA

As soon as my hotel door closes behind the bellhop, I throw my purse on the bed, walk to the window, and push the sheer curtain to the side. Manhattan's office buildings rise to meet the sunset sky in manmade majesty. I glance down at the sidewalk, seeing people hustling along the concrete in all directions. Add a million cabs flying by, and the entire scene has a crazed energy that makes it feel alive, like it has a pulse.

And to think, I almost didn't make it here.

I have one goal during my week here in the city: find a position that will provide enough money for me to live here permanently. It's likely a pipedream, since I just graduated from college and have limited work experience.

My best friend, Magnolia, a name that shouts born-in-the-south, which happens to be the case for us both, plans on joining me if I do indeed secure employment this week, so failure isn't an option. We've planned for years to take this city by storm, even if it means cutting each other's hair and living on ramen noodles to afford an apartment.

Leaning against the glass, I utter a quiet prayer that somewhere in this gritty, concrete jungle, my newbie résumé lands in the right hands.

I reach for my bag and pull out my cell phone along with a strip of foil packs—aka condoms. *What the hell?*

"*Maggie*," I mutter under my breath.

I drop the foil packs into a small trashcan by the dresser, bring up Maggie's number on my phone, and press call. We need to talk.

"Finally, Tessa! Are you there?" Maggie says in her usual high-octane speed.

"I found the condoms," I huff, though I'm not surprised. "What if my bag was searched at the airport and a TSA guy saw them?"

"He probably would've asked for your number. Loosen up, okay? What are your plans tonight?" she asks, skipping over the part where she needs to say she's sorry.

"I don't know." I wasn't crazy about venturing out for the first time alone as night settles over the city. There's a room service folder on the desk beside me, and I flip the cover over. "Maybe I'll order in." A quick glance at the prices makes me cringe and reconsider this choice.

"You've got to be kidding. Tessa, it's your first time by yourself in New York City! You need to do three things tonight."

"Give them to me." I sigh, knowing where she's heading. Nothing changes in her demands.

Maggie's been trying to get my cherry popped since high school. And for once, I have to agree with her. But I'm a realistic girl, and have watched every episode of *Sex and the City*, so I know finding a real love match in this place of non-committal relationships isn't going to be easy. I have to be open to the options, even ones I haven't considered before. However, one-night stands as a virgin are complicated. It's hard to hide those pesky hymens.

"Here's the plan," Maggie pipes in. "One: I want you to go downstairs to the hotel restaurant for dinner. No hiding upstairs with room service. Two: actually make conversation with a man, preferably the hot kind. Three: bring him upstairs and have awesome hotel sex."

I hear the glee in Maggie's voice. She must be picturing me calling her tomorrow morning to tell her I'd been plucked by some guy at the bar. So not happening. *Ever.*

"One, yes. Two ... maybe. Three, you're hilarious and crazy." I end with a laugh while shaking my head. "I've never had a random kiss, so why would you think I'd bring some random guy up to my room?"

"Live a little. No harm. No foul," Maggie singsongs her life's motto into my ear.

She's right. I should live, but does that mean grabbing the

first willing and able guy by the Gucci tie and dragging him upstairs?

"Believe me. I've been more than ready for a long time. But I have yet to meet a guy who measures up to being my V-card conqueror."

"You still have PTSD from those jerks at Montevallo," she says, mentioning the college we graduated from in Alabama a week ago. "Forget them. You're starting over in a new place. No one knows about your sex handicap or that your family's filled with policemen all over six feet tall."

"New city. New me," I say with all the enthusiasm I can muster, which isn't much considering the trauma I dealt with during college.

Once word circulated that I was still a virgin during my sophomore year, an invisible bull's-eye was placed between my legs. For three long years, I went out on a lot of first dates full of sweet talk and eager hands. No one wanted me for just *me*. They wanted bragging rights that they'd been my first. I shudder at the memories and pray they're buried back at the university. At times, I feel like the Eighth Wonder of the World. Someone has their work cut out with me … I hope.

"Change out of your jeans, put on some lipstick, and go downstairs. Do not stay in your room. Okay?"

"All right." After all, I didn't blow a hefty portion of my savings just to sit here on this bed and watch reruns of *Friends*. I came to New York City to try to find myself, and I need to walk out of this room to make it happen.

4

Ending the call with Maggie, I decide my Taylor Swift T-shirt and skinny jeans make me look like a fourteen-year-old fangirl, not a twenty-three-year-old woman. Determined to make myself presentable, I open my suitcase and find a pink dress with off-the-shoulder ruffle sleeves.

After quickly changing, I slip on a pair of nude pumps, coat my lips in a sheer pink lip gloss, and grab my bag. It's time to face my dreams head-on, even if they scare me more than I care to admit.

2

TESSA

Walking through the lobby, I take a deep breath as I approach the restaurant. The hostess is dressed in all black, making me second-guess my pink attire.

"Good evening. I'd like a table for dinner, if one's available," I say in a smooth, I-have-it-all-figured-out way. No need to expose my anxiety for being by myself in a city where I don't know a soul.

"Sure thing, miss," she says with a slight hiss. It stings a bit, but I brush it off. "Will your family be joining you?"

Ouch. That one hurt.

"No. Just me," I say, defeated by her words and feeling like a fifteen-year-old runaway.

After rolling her eyes at me, the bitchy hostess grabs a menu from under her stand, then leads me to a small square table.

"Your server will be with you shortly," she says, looking down her nose at me before turning away. *Good riddance.*

After settling into my seat, I glance around the restaurant. It has a definite Old World-meets-hipster vibe with its worn, polished tables and brick walls. Muted lights are strung high overhead, giving the space a dark ambiance. I picked Hammond Hotel because it was rated high on the trendy scale, and it definitely lives up to it.

I peruse the wine list, which consists of several pages, and concentrate on the reds served by the glass. I don't see a pinot noir or merlot anywhere, so I move to the sparkling wines, finally finding one that's familiar: my beloved prosecco. It's my version of champagne on a budget. A thirty-something man in a long-sleeved white shirt and black pants stops at my table.

"Good evening. My name is Jeffrey and I'll be your server." I give him a welcoming smile, which he returns. "Would you care for something to drink tonight?"

"Yes. May I please have a prosecco?" I respond, closing the catalog list of wines.

"Certainly," he answers, bending closer to me. "But I'll need to see your I.D."

At least he whispers the last part. Though, I should've expected it after the comments from the hostess. Seriously, it's surprising she gave me the wine list at all.

I pull my wallet from my purse and hand Jeffrey my Alabama driver's license. He scans it over, then appraises me, and finally smiles. *Whew.*

"I knew you were Southern, Contessa Holly," he says, giving me my license back. I don't miss the mischievous and flirty spark in his eye either. "And you have a beautiful first name. Fitting for a beautiful young woman."

"Thanks." I turn my eyes down toward my lap, feeling a flush spread across my face. I wonder if all men here are this forward.

"Do you go by Contessa?" he continues, though I wish he would go fetch my drink already.

"Just Tessa," I say, looking up at him once again.

Maybe in my thirties I'll try the older sounding version. I've always felt I needed to be more accomplished to wear my first name properly. Perhaps after I make senior executive, or get married and have a couple of kids. Though, at my pace, I'll be lucky to snag a first date.

"Tessa suits you. Be right back with a prosecco for the pretty lady in pink." He taps the table and gives me a not so subtle smirk before walking toward the bar.

I open the dinner menu and browse over the choices. My eyes go wide at the prices. All the entrees are over twenty-five dollars, even the usually less expensive pasta and chicken dishes.

The fact that I'm not in Alabama anymore hits me hard, and I realize a sobering truth: I need to land a job where I make some serious bank to survive here. I finally decide on one of the least expensive things: lentil soup. It should be filling and might include some bread, if I'm lucky.

As I wait for the server to return, an older man dressed in a rich dark suit enters the restaurant by himself, catching my attention. A suited man always turns my eye. It's my version of male lingerie.

His shoulders are broad and his stance is commanding. All eyes watch him stride through the restaurant like he owns the place. His thick, wavy hair is ink black with a glossy shine any woman would die for—myself included.

Forget the simple act of wearing clothes. His suit moves like it's upholstered to his form. Lucky suit. His pace slows as he approaches the bar, which happens to be close to my table. Lucky me.

His thick biceps flex as he pulls out a barstool and takes a seat. Dammit. Now his back is all I can see—not that I'm complaining. He has a really nice backside.

"Sorry for your wait, miss. Here's your drink." Jeffery seems out of breath as he places a champagne glass full of bubbling liquid in front of me.

"Thank you," I say before taking a sip.

As the cool liquid hits my tongue and quickly disappears, the handsome businessman twists on his barstool. He scans the room, stopping when his eyes land on me, meeting mine dead on.

Whoa ...

His piercing dark eyes regard me without expression. I freeze in place, my glass still touching my lips, finding it difficult to breathe. Good lord, he's the most beautiful man I've ever seen, aside from movies or magazines, and even then, I can't think of a guy hotter than him.

I turn in my chair and look behind me, fully expecting to find someone else standing there, like a beautiful woman worthy of his handsomeness. But the space is empty. I face forward again, my eyes reconnecting with this gorgeous stranger, overwhelmed he's giving me his full attention.

He shakes his head, and I notice a small rise at the corner of his full lips. The next thing I know, he gives me a dazzling smile, and a strange rush washes over me.

I think I just swooned and had my Jake Ryan *"yeah, you"* moment. Except the hot guy isn't a high school senior leaning against a sports car; he's a thirty-something suited sex god sitting at a bar in freaking New York City.

Glancing down at my dress, I grimace. The ruffle top reminds me of Molly Ringwald's bridesmaid dress in *Sixteen Candles*. Maybe it's time to upgrade my pretty-in-pink look.

I give him a weak smile in return, and consider this a monumental feat since I can't remember my own name. He brings a glass of amber liquid to his lips. His eyes never leave mine as he takes a sip, showing off his practiced seduction skills.

He licks his lips, and that devastating smile aimed right at me returns. My nipples react, trying to cut through the cotton of my thin dress. They've never met a man like this, or really any man, because he's nothing like the boys from college. He's a lethal and way-too-old-for-me man. *Maybe ...*

"Excuse me, miss. Have you decided on what to order?"

Jeffrey stands in front of me with a pen in his hand, blocking the eye candy who was eyeing me, thus destroying my swoony high.

"Oh yeah, order," I sputter as Jeffery waits for an answer.

"Yes, I'm assuming you're here for dinner, or maybe you're waiting on someone to join you?" His eyebrows rise in question.

"I'm sorry," I manage while sitting up in my chair. "May I please have the lentil soup?"

"And for your main course?" Jeffrey asks.

"Just the soup." *Ugh.* I need to find a place where I can eat a meal for less than fifty dollars.

"Another prosecco?" he asks, but I surely don't need more with my current brain buzz. Besides, I need to hit the sidewalks tomorrow morning in search of a job, not a hangover cure.

"No thanks. Just water."

With a quick nod, Jeffery slides my dinner menu under his arm and walks toward the back of the crowded restaurant.

Unable to resist the gorgeous man magnet, I turn back to find him still sitting sideways on the barstool turned toward me. He's focused on his phone, his long, capable fingers dwarfing it. Maggie has this crazy theory. She believes a man's penis is roughly double the size of his thumb, which would make this man extremely blessed below the belt.

His killer jawline has more stubble than a five o'clock

shadow, but he doesn't have a full beard. It would be a crime against Mother Nature and the humans in his presence to fully cover a jaw like his.

After a few minutes, he sets his phone down on the bar. With a slight smile, he picks up his drink and raises it in a toast … to me. I can't believe he's still looking my way. *What universe am I in?*

I raise my glass to match his and take a sip, but nothing meets my lips. I pull my glass away and eye it. *Empty.* He laughs at my situation, and I join him. He holds up a finger, asking me to wait, and swivels forward on his seat, signaling the bartender over to him.

During his conversation, he points to me, and the bartender nods before turning away. Mr. Tall, Dark, and Handsome gives me a big thumbs-up, so I guess he's buying me a drink? I can't believe this is happening. I owe Maggie for insisting I leave my room tonight. I never thought I'd make it past her first suggestion. Well, I haven't actually spoken to him, but buying me a drink is like saying hello in adult dating talk.

I mouth, "Thank you," and twirl a loose strand of hair around my finger—a nervous habit I've had since before I can remember, and one that makes me look childish. I tuck my hands under the table to control my errant fingers.

He grins at me with a quick nod, but there's something sweet in the way he looks at me. It calms me even though my heart is racing. When he pushes back from the bar and stands up with his drink in his hands, his clothes seem to magically fall in place around him. He doesn't need to even straighten his tie.

My breath catches as he moves toward me, and my heart rate hits aerobic levels. *Could he actually be coming over to my table?*

The idea both excites and freaks me out. Everything about him shouts worldly and refined, while I sit here in my Forever 21 dress looking like I just graduated from college … which I did.

Before he can take two full steps my way, a woman moves in front of him. *Dammit.* She's dressed in high-end couture with a tight black pencil skirt and a white silk blouse tucked in at the waist. Her dark hair is twisted into a high bun on top of her head. I can't see her face, but I watch her kiss him on the cheek, and sadly, he does the same to her.

They exchange a few words, and he glances over her shoulder to look at me. Our eyes lock, and he smiles while tilting his head, almost like he's trying to apologize. For what, I'm not sure. The woman turns her head, following his gaze to meet mine.

And of course, she's drop dead gorgeous, and closer to his age and level of sophistication. Perfect makeup, perfect hair, perfect clothes—the perfect polished look I'll never have this side of a Tim Gunn makeover and total submersion at Sephora.

With a knowing look in her eyes, the woman inspects me with that instinctual female once-over, then says something to him. He nods at her—or is it at me?

In complete shock, I can't seem to close my mouth. Here he is with a woman he's more than air kissed, and he's still flirting with me. What a player. A drop-dead gorgeous one, but a player is a player all the same.

The handsome jerk gives me a quick wink, then places his hand on the small of his date's back before guiding her out of the restaurant, making me question the short interaction I had with him.

I watch the cozy pair until they disappear into the lobby. It's a good thing his date arrived before he made it to my table. I'd rather know the truth from afar than have it blow up right in my face.

I take a deep breath and try to exhale all the crazy feelings this guy stirred up inside me. No man has ever gotten me this hot and bothered– or angry before. After two more breaths, I feel less revved up and notice Jeffrey heading toward me with a tray in his hands.

"Your lentil soup, my lady," he says, placing the steamy bowl down in front of me. "A basket of bread. I threw in a few extra pieces," he whispers.

"Thanks," I say, ready to dig in.

"And another prosecco from an admirer at the bar." He turns to where the man with the wandering eyes was sitting. "Well, looks like he's left. Odd."

"Yeah, very. Since he left with his date."

"Do you know who he was?" Jeffrey leans down closer to me, like he's telling me something he shouldn't.

"He buys me a drink before leaving with his date. I'd say

he's a cheater." I cross my hands over my chest with a huff. Just thinking about the gall of this stranger has me getting worked up all over again.

"No kidding?" Jeffery sets the tray down. "I've known him a few years. Actually, he owns this hotel ... well, his family does, and they're amazing to the employees here."

"Wait, he owns this hotel?"

"Yes, the Hammond family does. You know, the same ones who own Hammond Press?"

"What's his name?" I ask, because I've been trying to get this publisher to respond to my five hundred emails with my résumé attached. I think I've applied for every job they've posted online, even ones requiring ten years' experience. I want a job there badly.

"Barclay Hammond," Jeffrey says.

"You've got to be kidding me. I thought he was like seventy."

"Barclay Hammond Senior is, but the guy at the bar is his son, Barclay Junior."

"Wow." I've been reduced to one word, which is pretty sad considering I graduated with honors in English.

"Listen, I need to get back to my six-top." He picks up the tray and tilts his head to the right. "They keep looking my way and frowning."

"Sorry. Sorry," I say, shooing him away with my hands.

"Oh, by the way, he paid for your dinner."

"Really?"

"You must have made quite the impression on him," he adds, a sparkle in his eyes.

Even though this small bowl of soup and drink are double what it costs at home, it feels wrong accepting Barclay Hammond's payment knowing he's a typical Manhattan playboy.

I wish he'd come back so I can tell him what I think of him, then throw my prosecco in his handsome face and watch the drops dribble over his Armani tie. But it would be a shame to let my favorite drink go to waste.

3

BARCLAY

"Barclay." My sister, Victoria, sits across from me as we eat dinner at the Four Seasons in Midtown. I glance up from my now empty plate and see her regarding me with squinted eyes as she leans in her chair, her plate pushed toward the middle of the table. "You haven't said a thing to me in fifteen minutes while you inhaled your steak and frites."

"Sorry, sis. I've had a lot going on at work." The lie slips off my tongue.

I barely remember eating the food served to me and my distraction has nothing to do with work. It's the gorgeous creature I saw at the hotel bar after leaving the office. She reminded me how much I love the initial attraction and flirtation of meeting a woman—the addictive desire to pursue her and see if she feels the same electric chemistry buzzing between us.

My mind's been replaying the vision of the pink bombshell. It's a continuous loop that slows during my favorite parts, like when she looked over her shoulder in disbelief that I was paying attention to her. *How could I not notice her fresh beauty in a sexy pink dress?* It exposed the creamy skin of her shoulders, the blond waves tumbling over them. Damn, she was a sight.

I smile, thinking about the blush on her cheeks when she realized I was eyeing only her. I can't remember the last woman I saw blushing from simple eye contact.

She was old enough to drink, but way too young to handle a man like me. I'd likely break her heart and hate myself for it later. And the fact is, I don't have time to invest in a relationship. My every waking minute is spent working.

"Hmmm. I see," she says, gazing over her wine glass at me. "You know you just smiled—something you haven't done in months around me."

Damn, she caught me. I wipe the grin off my face as Victoria searches my eyes for the truth. My expressionless cover-up is likely useless, since I've never been able to hide anything from her, which gives her an unfair advantage. God knows I don't have a clue what's going through her mind, though I'm certain she's about to tell me.

"When was your last date?"

"I'm not ready for a relationship."

"I'm not talking about a girlfriend. A simple date. You know, those adult get-togethers for two that usually center around a meal and conversation?" She releases a frustrated sigh, setting down her wine glass. The topic belongs to her now, dammit.

With her black hair atop her head, serious blue eyes, and nosy questions, she resembles my mother, making me wonder if dear old Mom is somehow responsible for this intrusive discussion.

"How about dessert? They have a delicious flourless chocolate cake."

I could always distract her with sweets when we were growing up. If I hung a bag of gummy bears in her face, she'd forget about the heirloom china or crystal I'd break.

"Nice attempt at evading my question, but I worry about you not having a life outside the company." Her eyes soften, and she tilts her head. "It's been two months since you and Amanda split up. It's time to move on."

"It's weird. I really haven't felt any of the normal broken heart pains that go along with a breakup. After four years together, I should feel the loss, right?"

"Maybe you just didn't feel the *right* thing for her. After all, she gave you an ultimatum and you couldn't agree to it."

"It's not that I don't want to get married. It's just ..." I trail off, not knowing how to finish the sentence.

"That's what I'm getting at. She wasn't the one for you. It's not your fault. We can't help who we do and don't fall in love with. It either happens or it doesn't. But it won't ever happen if you don't date."

"My lack of dating has nothing to do with Amanda. It's more time related. I promise." I raise my fingers up in Scouts' honor. "I'm dedicated to taking Hammond Press to the next level in publishing. The book world is changing, and I don't want what Dad built to be left behind in the dust."

"Neither do I, but don't let work rule your life. You see what happened to Dad. At least he has us around for support."

I cringe at the topic. My father left Hammond Press a year ago when his doctors said his forgetfulness was more than him just getting older. I've tried to step in and take his place as CEO, but I have big shoes to fill. So far, the board of directors approve of my actions, and I plan on keeping them and our investors happy.

"I promise I'll get back in the game this summer. Maybe I'll meet someone in the Hamptons."

"Oh please, none of those phony types." My sister rolls her eyes, and I can't say I disagree with her. I want the woman I fall for to be genuine—not full of pretense and social climbing. Those kinds of women bore me after the first sip of champagne.

"You know me. I'm always looking for the diamond in the rough. And by rough, I mean the shallow pond of Manhattan's dating pool."

"Okay, you win. Let's change the subject. Mother wants

you to join them in Greenwich for Father's birthday in three weeks."

"I wouldn't miss it. I'll call her tomorrow with the news."

"Better get ready for her to grill you on bringing a date." Victoria laughs, but I know she's right. My mother wants what's best for me, and in her eyes, that's a wife and two kids.

"On second thought, why don't you just tell her I'm coming?"

"Not on your life, Barc. You need a little push. After all, you're inching closer to forty. And you know what they say about never-married men in their forties."

"No, but I'm sure you're about to inform me."

"They're commitment-phobes."

"Fine. I'll bring a date to Saturday's Warwick Awards and prove you wrong." My hands perspire as I tap my fingers on the table. I don't have time to worry about this, but my mother's persuasive tactics are worse than my sister's. I need the server to bring something sweet for Victoria to eat this instant. It's my only hope. "Just please tell Mom I'll be there in three weeks."

"I'll give you a pass this once, but if you're dateless, I'll pick a date for you for Dad's birthday party." She giggles, and I know I can't face whatever doomed date she's concocting, which will likely be with one of her friends. "Oh, there's one stipulation to this Saturday's date. She can't be anyone you already know. I want you to work for this one."

I've never been desperate enough to call an escort service,

though my lifelong friend, Trevor, swears by them. He uses the services when he needs a date to an event or a discreet hookup. If push comes to shove, I could call him for the number, but the thought makes my stomach turn.

You can't be more phony than a fake date, and knowing my sister, she'll see right through my ruse.

Basically, I'm screwed.

"One more thing. My and Danton's three-year anniversary is next week, and our nanny's mother has surgery. Can you watch Beatrice for us?" Her smile has a side of glee with it, meaning she already knows she's won this round too.

"I thought you wanted me to settle down, not scare the shit out of me. Hell, I've never changed a diaper in my life." My three-month-old niece is an adorable mini version of my sister, which means she also has an attitude. Heaven help me. "You can be quite evil."

"It's just a little reality check."

4

TESSA

When my phone alarm blares, I reach out from under the covers and search the nightstand in hopes of silencing the obnoxious sound. Without opening my eyes, I hit the screen a few times before the noise stops. *Hallelujah.* I hate mornings.

After a couple minutes, I open one eye as my sleep-infused brain tries to fire up. An unfamiliar gray wall with chrome fixtures fills my view, and it hits me: *I'm in New York City.*

I sit up straight in my bed and glance out the window. Last night, I left the curtains open with the twinkling lights of Manhattan serving as a nightlight. Now, my view is filled with shiny buildings catching the first glimpse of the sun.

I throw the covers off me and jump out of bed, heading toward the bathroom and getting my morning routine underway.

Forty-five minutes later, a doorman dressed in a tuxedo and top hat opens the door for me as I near him in the lobby. "Good morning, miss," he says with a serious expression. How can he be so somber on such a beautiful sunny morning?

"Thanks, sir." I can't hold back my smile, giving him a full-on grin, and the corner of his mouth twitches up. *Got 'em.*

I head outside the hotel onto the green-carpeted entrance. In front of me, a sophisticated woman climbs into the backseat of a shiny black town car and is whisked away. Cabs fly by with their honking horns. Even at this early hour, the city's energy is organized chaos.

Caffeine is my first priority, and according to the app on my phone, there's a Starbucks five hundred and thirty feet away. I love how the city measures distances to life's conveniences in feet versus miles. I won't even need a car to get around here.

I follow the little blue dot moving on my screen, making sure I'm heading in the right direction. When I pass by a mirrored storefront, I catch a full-length view of my reflection. My pink pencil skirt and white blouse combination may not be as tailored as the woman with Barclay Hammond last night, but it's not too far off. Thankfully, Maggie made me buy a few essential pieces for my job search, but I wouldn't budge on buying black. It may be the standard here in New York City, but it's also the color people wear to funerals back home.

The green goddess sign of caffeine appears ahead of me, and I pick up my pace. Once inside, I find the line ten people deep. The baristas are all business behind the counter, so the line moves quickly. Most of the customers exit the store, which leaves plenty of empty tables. Since I don't have a job to run off to yet, I find a seat by the window and text Maggie.

Call me if you're up.

Up.

I have to tell you about last night.

You met someone?

Maybe.

OMG. Calling.

"Hello," I answer after one ring.

"Who is he?" Maggie rushes out, and I can hear her coffee maker brewing in the background.

"Good morning to you, too. By the way, where were you last night?" I ask, because I called and texted her several times without a reply.

"On a date." She sighs. "I don't think he asked me a single question the entire night. I give up on finding a decent guy our age. They're consumed with making it big. All he talked about was making partner and buying a sports car."

"Tell me you didn't sleep with him."

"Nah. Just an oral exchange. It was a Tinder date."

"Maggie," I whisper-scream into the phone. "What were you thinking?"

"That all his talking gave him a wonderfully strong tongue."

"I can't believe you." We are such polar opposites in the sex and dating department. She's liberated and free thinking, whereas I've been stuck somewhere between second and third base since my senior year of high school.

"Hopefully you will understand what I'm talking about soon. Tell me about last night."

I recap the entire evening at the restaurant with Barclay Hammond. How he wouldn't stop staring at me, bought my dinner and drinks, then left with another woman. I leave out his connection to Hammond Press, and that I stalked him, for at least an hour, online after dinner.

The society pages mentioned he had broken up with a longtime girlfriend a couple months ago and he was one of New York City's most eligible bachelors. Oh boy, did he seem overly eligible last night.

"Damn, girl. What would you have done if he came to your table and his date never appeared?"

"I don't know. He was way too old for me."

"Like how old?"

"Maybe thirty-five or a bit older?" My voice trails off at the last part.

"Wow." She sounds as shocked as me. "That's the exact

type of man you need for your first time. Someone with experience, who knows how to make love to a woman. If you think those stares were too much, imagine what he could do in the bedroom."

"You have such daddy issues," I tease, but it's true. She would always point out the hot older man in the bars we snuck into in college.

"Remember that date I had with the silver fox?" Her dreamy voice floats away on a sex cloud.

"How could I forget?" My tone doesn't hide the irritation I still feel about listening to her brag. I tried to be happy for her, but I've never even had one orgasm with a man, let alone the scores she claimed occurred with a seasoned lover.

"Take it from me, Tessa. Older is better. They've learned their way around the equipment."

A shiver runs over my skin as I remember Barclay's eyes and how they bored into me. They had the look of knowing things about me even I wasn't aware of.

I imagine his full lips on mine, our tongues mingling while his long fingers touch me in places and ways I've longed to feel from a man.

"Earth to Tessa," Maggie nearly shouts.

"Huh? What?"

"I lost you somewhere after the orgasm discussion."

"Sorry. Still trying to wake up."

"Sure." Maggie laughs. "So, what's up for today?"

"I'm stopping at all the major publishing houses."

"Do you have an appointment or something?"

"I wish." Sighing, I sit back in my chair. "I have envelopes addressed to the human relations departments for each publisher and plan to leave them at their front desks. I can't seem to get anyone to answer my emails, so maybe a personal touch will be the ticket."

"You've got this, Tessa." There's nothing like having a best friend who believes in you more than you do in yourself.

"By the way, you were right about pink and this city. I look exactly like I arrived from the South." I glance around the coffee shop, appraising the customers. "It's a black sea with a few waves of gray mixed in."

"We've been over this. Do you like black?"

"Despise it."

"Then be your beautiful self in pink. Own it. Show those drab fuckers what it's like to swim upstream." Maggie knows all about being the anarchist. Me? I've always been happy to go with the flow.

"Thanks for the pep talk. I need to get a move on. Early bird and all. Plus, I only have a week to get a worm."

"In the form of a dick on a hot guy I hope."

"Stop." I giggle in an outside voice way, and a few people turn toward me with their mouths open in surprise. I guess laughter stands out in New York City as much as wearing pink.

5

BARCLAY

I take a deep breath as I pick up my cell phone. I'd rather have my chest hairs waxed than make this call, which is pure torture. Damn all the metrosexual grooming trends. A hairless man is like one of those hairless cats. They look naked and frightening as hell. A man needs to look like a man for fuck's sake.

Grumbling under my breath, I find the number I need and press call, wondering how to even begin this conversation. Kill me now.

"Barc," Lucas yells into the phone. Bells ring in the background, so he must be working on the trading floor. "Is everything okay? It's nine in the morning, and a workday. We rarely talk during daylight."

"Yeah, no emergencies or anything like that. Why don't you call me when you're off the floor." Even as I say the words, the noise in the background fades.

"I was just leaving that jungle. Getting the young guys set for the day. What's up?" Lucas gets right to the point, and I swallow before answering. I swore I'd never do this, yet here I sit in my executive chair about ready to do the unthinkable: pay for a date.

"Well," I say in a stalled response. "I need a number from you."

"A number? You know I can't give you any insider info on stocks. No perp walk for me, even for my closest friend. I will not be someone's bitch in a federal prison."

"Jesus, Lucas. I'd never ask for *those* kinds of numbers. I need a phone number." I pause a beat. "The escort one."

A bitterness lands on my tongue, but it's a pill I have to swallow because finding a date with a new woman by Saturday will be impossible with my workload.

"Wait a second. Did you say 'escort'?" Lucas's voice is filled with disbelief, and I feel the same way.

"Yes, it's a long story, revolving around my meddling sister, but I need a date for Saturday night. The Warwick Awards."

"Are you fucking with me, Barclay? It's only Thursday, dude. A guy like you could swing his briefcase and have a score of women willing to do just about anything with him— or for him."

"I'm not the same guy I was in my twenties." There's a reason I don't see my friend outside of the gym or sporting events. He still lives like he's twenty-five. "Maybe you know a specific woman who could work. She needs to be refined and real, not a Botoxed supermodel type."

"What gives?" Lucas asks. "You need to hang out with me tonight. There's this new place in The Village. We'll have this issue knocked out by nine, maybe sooner."

"Listen, forget I asked," I say, forgoing the crazy idea and hoping Lucas will forget this conversation ever happened. He has the memory of an elephant, so the chances are slim, but webs this tangled usually end up strangling someone in lies. The idea of going dateless and attending my father's birthday party with one of Victoria's friends sounds better and better by the moment.

"I have no idea why you need it, but it's yours. No questions. After all the jams you've helped me out of, I'll never be able to repay you. I'll even include the name of a girl you should request. Sending the text now."

"Thanks, but you know you're dead if this gets out."

"Hell, no one would believe the 'It' guy of the city would need an escort. Which worries me, dude. Let's get together Sunday. I have the company's box seats for the Yankees game. What'cha say?"

"Yeah, sounds good." A knock sounds on my office door, ending this distraction in my day. "Gotta run."

"Me, too. See you Sunday. And good luck with whatever happens."

"Thanks." We end the call, and I lay my phone face down on the desk, trying to put the unpleasant conversation behind me. "Come in," I call out, already knowing it's my assistant, Gail Mackenzie.

"Sorry to disturb you, sir, but do you need anything before the editorial heads' meeting?" My assistant has been with Hammond Press for forty years and could likely sit in my chair and run the place.

"You have everyone's coffee favorites, right?" Mrs. Mackenzie nods. "That should get the meeting rolling then."

She pulls out her phone and clicks away on it. "Order done. I'll be back in twenty, tops."

As she turns on her sensible heels to head out the door, I notice the pink scarf she's wearing. It reminds me of the young woman I saw last night whose beauty shined like the stars, practically blinding me. And for a split second, I consider wandering back to the hotel bar after work to see if she's staying there, but I think better of it.

Instead, I focus on my computer screen and read over the upcoming meeting's agenda. I try to convince myself she was a figment of my imagination—a mirage sent to distract my overworked mind—but I know she's real and likely too sweet for a "commitment-phobe."

I guess that leaves me with one option for Saturday night. And really, how bad could one escort date be anyway?

When my phone buzzes with an incoming text, I flip it over and view the message from Lucas.

He included the number and added a woman's name below it, but it's not the type of pink I was thinking about.

Ask for Barbie

6

TESSA

After I hang up with Maggie, my mother texts to check up on me. Yesterday morning, we said our goodbyes at my terminal in Birmingham's airport, and rivers streamed down her face. She swore they were happy tears and New York City would be lucky to have me, but her crackling tone told me otherwise.

I gave her a big hug and remained dry-eyed until I walked onto the plane. Completely out of her sight and soon to be lifting off Alabama's soil, my journey became real. An odd ache formed in my chest, as if the strained ribbon of child-hood connecting me to my mother had snapped. I sat in my seat, belted myself in, and had a good cry, thankful no one was sitting next to me.

My love of reading started with my mother. When she met my father, the town's sheriff, she had just become the librarian for Monroeville's small library. The lawman fell hard for the brainy beauty in the classic way opposites attract. While he patrolled the sleepy streets of our hamlet, she fed me a balanced diet of literature from birth.

Early on, I found a comfortable hiding place in between the pages of my favorite stories. So, when I gave up on boys in college, I returned to the familiar world of fictional men and women.

Needing a distraction from my lacking love life, I created a blog named after my late cat, Shakespurr, where I post book reviews all from finicky Shakespurr's point of view. Readers love it. He has quite the fan club. I even started selling shirts and mugs with his photo on them.

After the first few reviews, the blog gained a steady readership. I didn't quite go gangbuster viral, but I made money when people bought the books I posted via my marketing links.

My pile of college debt has dwindled down to a sane number, and I even stashed enough away to come to the Big Apple for seven days. I think Shakespurr would be proud of his human.

I reread the last text from my mother. *"Go confidently in the direction of your dreams."*

The famous Thoreau quote is just what I need as I head straight for Hammond Press. It's only a few blocks away from the coffee shop and even closer to my hotel.

Pacing along with the other people on the sidewalk, I double-check my bag to make sure the manila envelope with the letter and résumé addressed to Hammond Press is inside.

Since I've heard nothing but crickets from all the emails I've sent, I'll be happy to make it inside the mailroom doors at this point.

A nervous excitement races over my skin when the building comes into view. I shake the tingles from my fingers and walk faster.

The sidewalk traffic flow reminds me of a four-lane highway. Two slow lanes on each outer side, where people enter and exit the concrete highway. Currently, I find myself in the inner lanes moving at a high cruise speed.

Drawing closer to the building's entrance, I maneuver through the fast lines into the slow outer side, standing almost on the edge of the curb.

I swivel on my heels to face the glass and granite structure, and peer upward to see Hammond Press written in a bold marquee.

It's showtime. Butterflies scatter within me. I didn't think I'd have a major case of the chickenshits, but I do.

Dammit. I can do this.

Bringing my eyes back to the ground, I close them for a quiet moment to regroup, and resign myself to hoping I can push through my fear while still doing it afraid.

Two more deep breaths, and I open my eyes, my gaze still on the ground, where a shiny pair of men's black shoes mirror mine. The tips of our soles are separated by a few inches. I focus in, noting the perfect leather and sleek design of the men's version leans toward an expensive European brand.

I inch up the matching, black wool trousers, passing over a Gucci belt buckle and paper white dress shirt. A silk tie with woven threads of gray and black rests between the open lapels of a black suit jacket. Once past broad shoulders, I catch the man's tilted smile while his eyes catch all of me, slowly, from head to toe. He's not quite as tall, dark, and handsome as Barclay Hammond, but there's something similar in his look—and age.

"Pardon me, but you seem like you might need a little help," he says in a smooth tongue. His smile fades to concern as his fingers twitch, as if he wants to check my pulse. "Trevor Spears."

I give my head a slight shake before I reach toward his now extended hand. Mine disappears around his large fingers, and he holds his grip an appropriate second or two, though he lingers a second or two longer than appropriate on my boobs.

"Tessa Holly." My southern accent has a woman turning her head. Her eyes are wide, as if she's witnessing the sighting of an extinct animal.

"Where are you from, Tessa?" He pushes his suit coat to the side, settling his hand at his waist. I wonder if this is his relaxed pose.

"Take a guess." I add a swipe of sarcasm to my smile.

"Below the Mason Dixie line." He whistles as his eyes revisit my legs. He's so discreet. *Ugh.*

Nodding, I purse my lips and place my hand on my hip. He glances down at my mirrored move, and does this smirk laugh thing as he throws back his head.

"What brings you to the city?" His predictable questions are a breath of stale air.

I scoot to the right about six inches, so I can peek around his tall frame. The revolving doors at Hammond Press spin around as people come and go. I need to shake this man from my day and get on the circling merry-go-round.

"Actually, I was just headed into Hammond." I mark a way of escape and secure my bag onto my shoulder. Then, in stealth mode, I start to maneuver around him and re-enter the sidewalk highway.

"Remarkable, so am I." He turns to follow me, his large frame and giant strides clearing the walking traffic like a rope line, giving us a direct path to the front doors. "Do you work at Hammond?"

"No." Oh how I wish I could've said yes to this man. "I have a special delivery."

"Oh, you're a courier with a delivery from the South?"

"Something like that," I say out the corner of my mouth.

"Follow me. I know the security guard. No one and nothing gets past him without his approval."

"Thank you, sir," I say, addressing him in a proper

Southern way. I peer up into his eyes, wondering why they've become so dark. "I would greatly appreciate that."

"My pleasure." His response is smoother than velvet, and I have the weird feeling I've missed an element in our conversation.

Mr. Spears opens the single door next to the revolving one and places his hand on the small of my back, ushering me into the lobby. Though I've read about this gentlemanly contact in books, no man has ever led me this way. I do see the appeal.

The gray-colored marble lobby is longer than it is wide, and enclosed glass bookcases cover the sidewalls, rising two stories tall. Their shelves display scores of books, with the covers facing frontward. I recognize a few titles, even the most recent one from Don Black: *A Code for Mankind*.

My awestruck reactions make me fall a step behind Mr. Spears. I skip up next to him and reach the security desk as he does.

"Good morning, Mr. Spears," the guard welcomes my tall escort by name, substantiating his claim.

"Same." Mr. Spears is curt, not returning the warm greeting in full.

"What can I help you with, sir?" the guard asks.

"I have a special delivery for –" Mr. Spears raises his brows at me.

"Helen Ratner." I reach into my bag and pull out the manila envelope addressed to her. "She's the head—"

"Of human resources," Mr. Spears interrupts, looking at me with a laugh in his eyes.

I realize there's only one way he could know Helen's position within the company. The Gucci devil works here too.

Mr. Spears takes the letter from my hand faster than I can react and passes it to the guard. "Please see that Helen gets this ASAP. Make sure to tell her I asked you to deliver it."

Mr. Spears holds up one finger to the guard, making all of us still, then gazes down his nose at me.

"Hmmm," he hums in thought, his single digit suspended in the air. "What's your favorite position?"

I gasp, glance at the guard, who has his mouth open, then look back at Mr. Spears. He curls his lip and shakes his head as the blanks begin to fill in.

Calling him sir. Dark eyes. Talk of positions. Snide smirk.

He's totally coming onto me, but I need a break to get through the company's guarded door. It's the age-old dilemma for women, and one I've stood against.

"Here at Hammond, I mean. What position would you like?" he asks the right question, but way too late.

I silently apologize to Gloria Steinem before answering him. "Publicity or marketing."

"Perfect," he responds before turning back to the guard. "Get on it."

The guard hustles through a door on the back wall, and another guard in the wings takes his place.

"I'd be happy to give Helen a call later today. Make sure

she received your letter." Mr. Spears places his hand back on the small of my back and guides me toward one of the enclosed glass bookshelves.

"You would?" I study his face, deciphering his level of sincerity. The Big Bad Wolf glint in his eyes tells me everything.

I step away from him, breaking the contact of his hand with my lower back, and a woman shouts, then something bumps into me near my shoulder blades. Before I make a full turn, cold and hot liquids pour down my back.

"Oh my gosh. I'm so sorry. I couldn't move out of your way fast enough," the woman says frantically, a drink tray of toppled Starbucks cups in her hands. All Venti.

She thrusts the caffeine catastrophe at Mr. Spears. His eyes are planted on my backside, and not for untoward reasons. He appears stunned, speechless, as he takes the dripping mess in his hands.

"Thank God I grabbed these with the coffee," the woman says, fisting a pile of napkins. "Did you get burned?" she asks, rubbing and pressing the napkins over my back.

"No. More cold, actually," I reply, still in shock.

"Good. The cold brews are what got you the most. My sincere apologies, dear."

The woman proceeds to shake the remnants off my shirt and continues to wipe it clean. She mutters under her breath and bows her head. I don't think it's looking good, but I can't see my back fully to be certain.

"We need to get this taken care of before the stains set in.

Do you mind coming upstairs with me? I'll send your clothes out for a quick cleaning. I think I have a trench coat for you to wear while you wait."

"Can I join you?" Mr. Spears asks as the coffees continue to spill over the tray onto the floor.

"I don't think that's a good idea, Mr. Spears," the woman answers, gathering me to her side. "Please just throw the coffees away and get housekeeping down here."

"Already on it, Mrs. Mackenzie," the replacement guard yells from his desk.

"At least one male is being useful," she says, whispering under her breath so only I can hear. I giggle for a beat.

I like this woman, even if she ruined my blouse, and likely my skirt too. Besides, she's taking me upstairs, way beyond the lobby and my wildest dreams.

"My boss will just have to do without the fancy coffee for his meeting," she says, walking me toward a bank of elevators. "Mr. Hammond will understand, though."

"Barclay Hammond?" the question rushes from my lips.

"Yes. I'm Alice Mackenzie, Mr. Hammond's assistant. What's your name, dear?"

"Tessa Holly, ma'am."

"Well, I'll have you back on your way in short order. Promise." Her kind eyes warm away some of my shock.

Once in the elevator, Mrs. Mackenzie hits the button for the highest floor. The numbers over the door fly by as we move closer to the handsome suited player who bought my dinner and drinks last night. My stomach twists in a knot. Will he remember me? There's no way I'll ever forget a man like him.

7

BARCLAY

The five head editors for Hammond Press are gathered around a large rectangle table in the boardroom connected to my office, and I sit at the head, presiding over an emergency meeting.

Don Black, our company's prized author, has been missing in action for two weeks—something he's never done in the fourteen years we've published his books. If anything, he and his agent are high maintenance, communicating almost daily, requesting numbers or extra publicity.

"I've called his agent two or three times a day. Sent emails too. All unanswered. It's like he's ghosting me." Marcus Gunderson, my editor-in-chief, wipes sweat from his forehead, as if he just finished a marathon. The dark circles under his eyes and ashen complexion make him appear ten years older. "His agent says he's, and I quote, 'taking a break.' *What the hell does that even mean?"*

"There can only be one answer. Another publisher is trying to lure him away from us. Our company depends on him. Hell, all of us do." I glance around the table, stopping to look at each of them. "Those nice vacations you all take during August? The checks you write to your kids' prep schools? Well, kiss them goodbye if he jumps ship to one of our competitors."

Marcus turns white as a sheet of copy paper. He has two sons at The Dalton School on the Upper East Side, where the tuition is over forty thousand a year.

"I'm at a loss." Marcus runs shaky fingers through his brown hair. "I'll try his agent again after the meeting."

"At this point, we don't have a firm answer on whether he's attending the Warwick Awards this weekend, correct?" I ask as my jaw tightens. "He has to be there. Rumors are circulating that he's won book of the year."

Marcus shakes his head while all the other editors avoid eye contact with me. I give my employees plenty of space to do their job, but I demand excellence and pay them accordingly. And when I feel like they miss the damn mark, there's a price to pay.

It's not just about the money the company loses. It's about people's lives. How they feed their children. Pay their mortgages. One mistake can have an avalanche effect on the entire company.

"We need an answer today." I rub the back of my neck, feeling the weight of the company's future pressing heavy on my shoulders. "Losing Black isn't an option."

Silence lingers, making one thing crystal fucking clear: no one has a plan for reaching Black.

"Marcus, you have until five o'clock to get a yes from either Black or his agent, or else." I rise out of my chair, towering over the table. "And believe me, you don't want to know what 'or else' means. Now, get to work. The meeting's adjourned."

"Understood, Mr. Hammond." The fact that Marcus called me by my surname further drives home the point. His neck is on the line, and he knows it.

The editors gather their belongings in quick fashion before scrambling out of the room. I walk over to the window, needing a few minutes to reflect on the repercussions of Black leaving. Nothing is forever in this business, and hell, we've published him for fourteen years—an eternity in today's fickle business climate of reaching for the biggest brass ring.

Leaning a hand high on the window, I gaze out at the shining copper building across from Hammond Press. It houses our largest competitor, Seamen & Schilling, with Mort Tuckerman sitting on the penthouse floor as CEO.

He's tried to end our company countless times over the years, and I can't help but wonder if he's behind Black's lack of communication. My blood boils at the thought of him winning over our prized client.

I can't fail, and it's not just about my own ego getting bruised. Hammond Press's success or misfortune will be my father's legacy. He poured his life into making this company a publishing trailblazer.

I will not fail him, and in the end, the company's fate lies in my hands. I need to handle this potential catastrophe myself.

I push off the glass window and head out of the conference room knowing what I have to do to handle the problem. Forget the unanswered phone calls and ignored emails, it's time to knock on Don Black's front door.

His home is in Greenwich, Connecticut, just over an hour away, and as a self-professed hermit, Black only ventures out on special occasions. If he won't answer his door, at least I gave it a try.

If only I had something in hand to lure him out of hiding. Maybe a chocolate cake from the bakery across the street would do the trick. Black doesn't seem like the type for sweet frosted cupcakes. First, I need to order the car and have Mrs. Mackenzie sort out the dessert.

Entering my office suite, I come to a dead stop. Mrs. Mackenzie stands near my desk, but she's not alone. Right beside her is the blonde bombshell from last night—the one I swore to avoid at all costs.

Forget the pink ruffled dress that exposed her soft skin. This time she's wrapped in a leg-baring khaki coat with a belted waist showcasing hourglass curves. Hell, she's standing in my office like a fantasy stripper here to entertain me.

I blink a couple times, not believing what I see, but nothing changes. She's still there, gazing at me with bright blue eyes and glowing porcelain skin, making her look even more young and beautiful up close.

Hell, is she even twenty-one? Not that it matters. Either way, I'm too old for her.

Helpless to stop my feet, I move to her like a black magnet to shiny steel, needing to know what the hell she's doing in my office, besides being a distracting dish of temptation, making my better judgment melt away. For all I know, she's a spy for the enemy next door. Though, I highly doubt Mort would deliver a beauty like her to me. He'd more than likely keep her for himself.

"Hello again." I can't stop the rare smile that crosses my face. "Barclay Hammond."

I extend my hand, and she reaches for it. Her soft and delicate fingers fit into my grasp like a matching puzzle piece. A small shiver passes through her touch—a vulnerable and dangerous revelation.

No one would call me a wolf, at least not to my face, but I've never been labeled as an angel either.

8

Standing in the presence of this handsome man, with his curious smirk, all the anger I have for his behavior melts away. I try to remember the words I wanted to tell him when he walked out of the restaurant after secretly buying my dinner, but nothing comes bubbling up in my mind.

I have hormone-induced amnesia and finally understand how scoundrels get away with their actions. If I looked in the mirror, I'd likely see cartoon stars in my eyes. I couldn't be more predictable if I tried.

"Tessa Holly," I whisper in response to his greeting, trying to decide whether this is a dream or reality. Never in a million years did I think my first day of job hunting would land me in the CEO's suite.

I glance from Mr. Hammond's strong, handsome face to our connected hands. The touch between us tingles ... or maybe that's just me reacting to this man. Either way, I've already looked beyond last night without even demanding an explanation. It's impossible to be angry when eyes like his scan over me, or a jawline shows such proud strength. Instead, I probably resemble a swoony dollop of meringue.

"We meet again, Miss Holly." My name rolls off his tongue as he releases my hand. "It's not every day I have encounters like this in my office."

"You two know each other?" Mrs. Mackenzie glances back and forth between the towering titan and me.

"In a roundabout way, we met last night at Hammond Hotel," he replies with an sly turn of his lip. Mrs. Mackenzie gasps, and I can only imagine what she's thinking. The man has no shame. "Right, Miss Holly?"

And how do I respond to him? Pathetically, by giving him a slow nod as my lips form a silent O. Plus, my hand is still tingling from his touch, and my dormant nipples have been brought to life. Such traitors.

"What's going on?" Mr. Hammond lifts his hand with an upward palm as his eyes shift between Mrs. Mackenzie and me. "It appears there's something up between you two."

"Well ... there was an accident with the coffees for the meeting. My apologies for not delivering them on time, by the way." Mrs. Mackenzie flutters her hands in the air.

Our incident in the lobby seems to have thrown her for a loop, or perhaps it's the strange electricity buzzing in the room.

"Coffee wouldn't have helped this morning anyway," he says with a frown while looking between Mrs. Mackenzie and me. My skin heats up as his eyes wander over my body. "What do you mean by accident?"

"I was walking through the lobby with your coffee order, and out of the blue, I ran into Miss Holly. She was covered in lattes and cold brews." Mrs. Mackenzie turns toward me with an apologetic smile in her eyes. "She's wearing my spring coat while I have her outfit dry cleaned. You should've seen the mess."

"That explains a few things, but I'm curious about something." Mr. Hammond rubs his chin in thought, his eyes twinkling. "What brought you to our building, Miss Holly? Following me perhaps?"

"What?" I sputter, not prepared for this question. The man thinks I'm stalking him like some desperate female. Okay, so I did stalk him online for an hour, maybe two, but I didn't come here for any other purpose than to drop off my résumé.

"Maybe you wanted to thank me for picking up your tab last night." Mrs. Mackenzie gasps even louder than before, but I can't look away from Mr. Hammond and his know-it-all, smug face.

My cheeks heat up into a color likely matching fuchsia. Who does he think he is? Something inside me shifts gears, and I know my mouth is about to get me in trouble. Time to stand up for womankind.

"Thanks for the dinner," I spit out, moving closer to him with my hands on my hips. The hem of the short trench coat moves higher up the front of my naked thighs, and Mr. Hammond's gaze doesn't miss it either. Cocky man even licks his lips.

I mentally do a windup for my next pitch below the belt. "Wonder what your date would've thought about it?" The sexy smirk disappears from Mr. Hammond's face, replaced by a creased brow. I can't wait to hear how he talks himself out of this mess, though his stern face, with its hard lines, is rather delicious.

I bite my lower lip to keep myself from licking it. I sure as heck don't want to mirror him or resemble the heroines in my romance novels—those silly women who succumb to lovers by a mere look. That will never be me. Ever.

I take a step backward, needing distance, but Mr. Hammond moves forward. And poor Mrs. Mackenzie clears her throat.

"Your sister, sir?" Mrs. Mackenzie speaks in a soft voice, tilting her head slightly. A light sparks in Mr. Hammond's coal colored eyes.

"Oh, right." He throws his head back with a laugh. My, what a powerful neck he has. "The woman you think was my date is actually my sister, Victoria."

I remember the woman having matching hair color and even a similar skin tone. He didn't kiss her directly on the mouth either, just familiar pecks on the cheek. I screwed up. It's time for me to grovel and get escorted back to the lobby —where I belong.

"I totally jumped to a conclusion based on what I saw, Mr. Hammond." He gazes at me with dancing eyes, seeming to hold back a laugh. "Please accept my apologies. Also, I need to *truly* thank you for my dinner. It was very kind, sir."

I know when to admit my mistakes. I can almost hear my mother cheering in the background.

He straightens and places his hands on his hips. I catch the strain of his tailored white shirt over his chest. He appears so intimidating and tall compared to my petite frame.

"No harm." He sticks his large hands in his pant pockets and rocks on his feet. The fabric strains against his thighs, like there's a solid sheet of granite beneath the dark navy wool. "It was my *pleasure*, actually. Shame I couldn't have joined you, though."

I bring my hand to my throat, maybe to check my rapid pulse. *When did my breathing become so shallow?*

"Me too," I manage to say. It's a small miracle, because this beautiful man, and his sexually charged attention, makes me dizzy. Who knew I'd meet a man who made it difficult to just stand in his presence?

"We should let you get back to work, sir." Mrs. Mackenzie touches me lightly on my arm.

"Actually, I need your help." Mr. Hammond turns toward

Mrs. Mackenzie, a work mode expression on his face. "Have my driver here in twenty minutes."

"Do you have an appointment downtown? I didn't see one on your calendar."

"Cancel all my meetings today. I'm going to visit Don Black up in Connecticut."

"Don Black," I blurt out in a rush. Mr. Hammond and Mrs. Mackenzie look at me, and I realize I've interrupted them with my silly fangirl enthusiasm. "Sorry. He's one of my favorite authors."

"You have something in common with Hammond Press. He's this company's favorite author too." Mr. Hammond's tone is firm, without the adoration I exhibited.

"I'll text the driver. I believe Lawrence works on Thursdays. Anything else?"

"Black's ignoring our calls, so I need to bring him a peace offering. Maybe a chocolate cake from the bakery across the street. Anything to get me past the front door."

"I know what you should bring him," I pipe up, unsolicited, and both of them turn my way.

"You do?" Mr. Hammond regards me with narrowed eyes. The skeptical kind that need to be put in their place. Here goes.

"I do." I nod my head in confidence, standing a little taller. My shoulders shake with a little sass.

"And how would you have gathered this information about a man who's been on the New York Times since before you were born, not to mention his Pulitzer Prize for Fiction?"

Mr. Hammond sure thinks he knows everything when he actually has no clue about his own client's likes. My explanation should be rather embarrassing, but he did ask for it.

"Off Mr. Black's blog. You do read his daily posts? After all, he's your favorite author." I press my lips together to keep from blasting a "gotcha" smile. No need to gloat.

"Okay, Miss Holly." Mr. Hammond rubs the back of his neck and takes a deep breath. "Be a good girl and tell me what he prefers."

I wonder if it's bad that I like him calling me a good girl, because it makes me feel weak-kneed. Probably, but I smile sweetly at him anyway. *How many switches can one man flip?*

"Don Black loves cherries in everything, especially his sweets. He discusses this weakness at least once a week." I tap my chin in thought. "A cherry pie is too predictable. I vote on bringing him a cherry tart."

"Perfect." Mr. Hammond reaches into his back pocket and pulls out a Gucci wallet. *What is it about that designer and the hot men working at this place?* He opens it up, removes a black credit card, and hands it to me. I take it, of course, though I have no idea why. "Run across the street to Sweet Nothings and pick out a cherry anything."

"Okay." I can't say no, but my answer is less than enthusiastic. I'm wearing a borrowed coat, that exposes too much of my legs, and I need to wait a couple hours for my clothes. This entire interaction feels like a comedy of errors.

"Mrs. Mackenzie, when will Miss Holly's clothing be back from the cleaners?" Mr. Hammond stuffs his wallet back into his pocket, the card matter and my assignment a thing of the past.

"Two hours, tops." Mrs. Mackenzie clicks away on her phone, deep in concentration. The woman's fierce. "Driver is secured. He'll be here in twenty minutes. It's the black sedan. Escalade's in for service."

"Thanks." Mr. Hammond walks behind his desk and shuffles a few papers on it. Then he glances up and scans me from head to toe. I swallow a breath. If only I knew what he was thinking.

Do I leave for the bakery now? It's all so confusing.

"What are your plans today, Miss Holly?" Mr. Hammond's commanding voice makes my mind mush. But, oh my God, why is he asking about my day? How should I answer him?

I do have plans to continue my job search, but those can change on a dime for a CEO like him—or just him in general. After all, Hammond Press is my first choice, though he has no idea I even dropped off my résumé. I need to use my limited acting skills and play it cool. I don't want to appear overanxious or nervous.

"Well …" I pull my cell from the trench coat pocket and pretend to scroll over my screen. The thing isn't even unlocked, but he'll never know it. "Let me see." I pretend to scroll some more. "I can rearrange things so I'm free." I place my cell back in the pocket.

"Great. You're going with me to Black's house."

"I am?" I squeak out in total shock, my eyebrows skyrocketing.

"You are." Mr. Hammond lasers his eyes on me. I nod, because there will be no denying him with that look, as if I would anyway.

"She is?" Mrs. Mackenzie shakes her head. "But—?"

Mr. Hammond interrupts her before she finishes. "I need to talk with Black. *Today.* A cherry tart delivered by her in a trench coat is a sure bet for him opening his door." He rounds his desk and walks toward me, but my mind is still spinning. "Now, run along. Meet me in front of the building after you finish at the bakery."

"Yes, sir." He gives me this huffed smirk, and small bumps rise across my skin.

Overwhelmed by this entire interaction, I manage to exit the office suite and throw my hands up in the air. *How is this my life?* I have to call Maggie. She's never going to believe what's happening to me.

9

TESSA

The baker assures me he has the city's finest cherry tart hot out the oven, and while I wait for the treat to cool down, I find my phone at the bottom of my bag. A rundown on my current situation with Maggie will take more than a few texts, so I call her instead.

When I give her the details of the entire morning, she hardly interrupts my flow or asks a single question, which shocks me. Finally, I have a story so exciting and crazy, Magnolia Talbot is speechless. I need to mark this day in my calendar and celebrate it annually.

"So, the hot CEO wants you to be his cherry tart and take

you for a little drive. Sounds like he has a food kink." Maggie loves teasing me and making me uncomfortable, so I keep my feelings about how much our sexual tension filled his office to myself. If she finds out how attracted I am to him, she'll overnight condoms to replace the ones I found in my suitcase.

"Stop it. I was in his office with his assistant. There's nothing going on like that."

Or is there?

I remember how he let his eyes browse over my entire body. The intensity on his face was scorching hot. The memory gives me a rush, but we are leagues apart, not to mention years. He was likely learning how to drive at the same time I was starting to walk. Talk about a sobering slap in the face.

"Bet he'd be okay if there was something up with you two. Did you at least ask him for a job?" I hear the anxious-ness in her voice, and I understand why.

We're both depending on me making it happen. It's a lot of pressure, to be honest, and makes me wonder if I should've declined Mr. Hammond's offer and continued my job hunt today.

"I can't ask the CEO for a job. Anything I'm qualified to do at his company would be so far down on the totem pole from him. Think mailroom or copy girl. He'd have no clue if the position was even available. And if he did find me a job, I'd always be the girl *he* helped. You know how people talk. They'd think it was a trade-off between us."

"Oh, you mean like you blew him, and he wanted you working under him?" Maggie roars in laughter.

I flush at her comment, then fan myself as I imagine really being beneath him. My short daydream comes to an end when his tie falls in my face as he hovers over me. Even my fantasies are lame.

"Miss?" the man assisting me at the bakery draws my attention. "Your cherry tart is ready."

"Oh, Maggie. I need to let you go. I have to pay." I place my trusty bag on the counter and dig for my wallet. "I'll text you later."

"Have fun. And by fun, I mean steam up the windows in the backseat. I'm sure his driver has seen it all." She laughs, and I roll my eyes. Then it hits me: I'll be sitting in the backseat next to Mr. Hammond for miles.

What will we talk about? Suddenly, it's hard to breathe. Plus, he's a giant-sized man and will take up most of the seat. I'll have nowhere to escape from him. My skin itches under the starchy coat. I hope I don't break out in hives.

I toss the phone in my purse and hand the man Barclay's credit card. For the first time in my life, I need a drink—preferably a couple. I glance over the bakery menu and see a familiar friend: mimosa. I want to blow it a kiss.

"Can you add two mimosas to that charge?" I should ask Mr. Hammond before I voluntarily make him pay for liquid courage, but I'll just rationalize it as my cost of labor for helping him. My father, the sheriff, would call it stealing. I hate moral dilemmas so early in the morning.

"Two, miss?" I nod and peek out the window, wondering if Mr. Hammond's car has arrived yet. There's only a standard yellow cab dropping off a passenger, but I do see a familiar man walking into the bakery. It's Trevor Spears, the résumé helper from the lobby. Once on the other side of the door, he spots me ... or more like my legs with his tongue hanging out and eyes bugged. A smirk of approval slides across his face, but it has the opposite effect as Mr. Hammond's.

"What happened to your clothes—or should I ask?" Again, he tiptoes on the border of inappropriate. Mr. Spears leans against the glass case beside me. I hope he doesn't leave prints on the glass or a layer of grease, because this is one slick guy.

"The coffee. Remember?"

"Oh, yeah. I was distracted," he says while gazing at me, or more like my boobs. *Gross!*

"Miss, here's your order." The smiling bakery helper hands me a sturdy paper shopping bag with handles on each side. "I need you to sign this first."

A slip of paper and pen lay on the counter in front of me. *How the heck do I sign this?*

"Just a second, Mr. Spears." I grab the pen and scribble something down on the signature line. Actually, I write a big fat lie of a name.

Mrs. Barclay Hammond.

I pray Mr. Hammond doesn't ask me for a receipt.

"Miss, we can't give you to-go cups for the mimosas. I'm

afraid you'll have to drink them inside," says the crestfallen worker. They truly aim to please here.

"That's perfect." I wave off any concern, and the bakery guy smiles in relief. "Do you like mimosas, Mr. Spears?"

"Usually not this early, but I'm a man of exceptions." And there goes that grin of his again. It doesn't take a psychic to read his dirty mind.

"Great," I say, turning toward the bakery man and taking the mimosas from his hands. I hand one to Mr. Spears and lift the other. "Cheers."

I consume the drink like a champagne shot. Mr. Spears eyes me in amusement as I hand my glass back to the man behind the counter.

Mr. Spears follows my lead, tossing back his, and then sets his glass down on top of the glass, likely leaving drippings all over the place. The man has no consideration for the workers who keep the displays spotless. Speaking from his experience as the town sheriff, my father always said one's true character is revealed by how they treat those who work service jobs.

Remembering what brought me to this spot, I glance out the window. Mr. Hammond owns the pavement while taking long strides toward a large black sedan—the one I need to meet him at now. Time to make my fast escape.

"Sorry, Mr. Spears. I have to run." I gather the bag containing the cherry tart and adjust my handbag. "Duty calls."

"Wait," he calls from behind.

I attempt to walk away without another word as my heels make staccato clicks on the tiled floor. I reach out to grab the door handle, but Mr. Spears beats me to it. I suck at quick getaways.

"Here, at least let me get the door for you." He pulls the handle, and I exit the store.

Outside on the sidewalk, I stop dead in my tracks when my gaze meets Mr. Hammond standing tall next to the black car. His eyes go wide as Mr. Spears places his unwelcomed hand on my lower back.

Before I can react, someone calls out from behind me, and I glance over my shoulder.

"*Mrs. Hammond*," the man shouts over the busy street noise, "you forgot your credit card."

Oh, shit.

10

TESSA

Mr. Spears gasps as I take the black credit card from the bakery guy. *How the hell am I going to explain this one?*

"Is that Barclay Hammond's card?" I give him a quick nod and walk as fast as my legs will carry me on the sidewalk. From across the street, Mr. Hammond peers at me with narrowed eyes, then glances between Mr. Spears and me. His jaw tightens into a knot of disapproval.

"That guy called you Mrs. Hammond. What the hell is going on?" Mr. Spears grabs hold of my arm. We're stopped at the crosswalk, and the light tells me I can't cross, so I'm stuck.

"Nothing, okay." He has some nerve touching me. I shake

his hand off my arm and wait for the light to change. "I just ran an errand for him."

"Wow. You went upstairs to his office, and now you're fetching him food in a sexy coat. Are you already working for him as his special assistant?" He ends his question with a creepy laugh.

"No." There's no easy or sane way to explain how I've found myself standing in this very spot, mainly because I don't understand it myself. "Will you do me a big favor?"

"Maybe." Mr. Spears' grin relays that any agreement from him will come at a price. "What are you hiding?"

"Don't tell Mr. Hammond I dropped off my résumé," I beg him. I don't want to get a job at Hammond Press because the CEO told someone to hire me. I want to earn a job on my own merit.

"I'll act like I've never met you before on one account." Mr. Spears' attempt to make his voice sound seductive has the opposite effect, but I need his cooperation. Plus, time's running out to get him to agree with me.

"What do you want?" I roll my eyes as the crosswalk light changes and make my way across the street with Mr. Spears at my side. I purposefully keep my eyes turned away from Mr. Hammond's glare.

"Meet me for drinks tomorrow night." Mr. Spears doesn't ask, he demands.

"Okay, but only drinks." I'd rather have a tooth pulled, but I don't see a way around it.

"Name the time and place." I breakout in the heebie-jeebies after Mr. Spears once again touches me, placing his hand on my lower back. Thankfully, we're approaching the waiting town car. Mr. Hammond stands beside it, his arms crossed over his chest. His pursed lips worry me.

"Eight thirty at the Hammond Hotel." I finish just out of Mr. Hammond's direct earshot. I hope.

Mr. Spears leans closer to me, if that's even possible. "See you tomorrow, Mrs. Hammond," he whispers into my ear. His hot breath blows against my skin. How could he smell like garlic before noon? Yuck.

I need to schedule a sudden migraine tomorrow night after our first drink—or earlier.

"Hello, Barclay," Mr. Spears addresses Mr. Hammond with an odd wave type salute and heads toward the entrance of the building without waiting for a reply, leaving me standing by Mr. Hammond holding a bag and my breath.

I crane my neck to meet Mr. Hammond's eyes. He towers over me in a wall of Armani. How can any man be this gorgeous? I had no idea it was humanly possible until meeting him. I bite my lip to keep from sighing.

Regarding me from head to toe, Mr. Hammond opens the sedan's door. "Be a good girl, Miss Holly, and get in," he says in a commanding tone. So much for a warm hello.

I wonder if his sour attitude has anything to do with Mr. Spears. There didn't seem to be anything warm and fuzzy in their interaction. I hope that's the reason for his ticked off attitude.

"Yes, sir." My southern manners kick in and I try to climb

into the car, but wearing this short trench coat makes it nearly impossible to be ladylike. I tug down the hem and pray Mr. Hammond doesn't get a view of anything private.

Once seated in the car, I slide over toward the window, holding the edges of the coat in place. The soft leather of the seat caresses the backs of my legs, all the way up to my panties. Outside of wearing a swimsuit, I've never exposed so much skin in public. My mother would be livid, and my father would have Mr. Hammond cuffed and bent over the car, likely asking about his intentions with me.

In one fluid motion, Mr. Hammond folds himself into the backseat as I gape at him in awe. His every move stirs a craving inside me I don't recognize, making him lethal to my virtue.

Once he's sitting next to me, his long legs spread to give him more room, taking up the empty space between us. I have no idea where to place the bag with the cherry tart in it, so I set it on top of my naked legs. The tart feels warm against them.

After Mr. Hammond shuts the door, his cologne fills the air, reminding me of the fresh pines in the forest near my home—clean, woodsy, and masculine. A couple more breaths later, and there's a good chance I won't survive the ride to Don Black's house. He smells divine.

"Lawrence," Mr. Hammond addresses his driver, sitting in the front seat. "Please place this up front. Also, can you check the trunk for a blanket?" He takes the sack off my lap and passes it through the divider to his driver.

"Certainly, sir." His driver exits the car and walks to the trunk.

I don't understand why he's asking for a blanket in May, especially since the car feels warm with his body heat radiating all around me.

"Are you friends with Mr. Spears?" Mr. Hammond demands. He balls the fist resting on his strong thigh and releases it. His neck muscles strain as he awaits my answer.

"We only just met today outside your building." Thankfully, I don't have to lie, though I do omit some of the truth—and the fact that I have a drink date with the man in question.

"A word of warning. Stay clear of him," he cautions with a sideward glance, and I nod.

Mr. Spears comes across as a big creeper. Meeting him tomorrow night sounds like a big mistake. *How did finding a job become so complicated?* I never thought I'd have to maneuver between two men.

The car shakes when the driver returns to the front seat and shuts his door. "Sorry, sir. There isn't anything in the trunk."

"Thanks for checking." Mr. Hammond mutters something else under his breath. I love watching his full lips move, though I can't make out what he's saying. "Mrs. Mackenzie gave you the address, correct?"

"Yes, Mr. Hammond. It's plugged into the GPS," the driver responds, pulling the car into busy Manhattan traffic.

Hardly a minute passes before Mr. Hammond twists and

turns in his seat, attempting to remove his suit coat. His wrestling act takes up even more space in the backseat, so I move closer to the window to give him more room.

Once he's out of his jacket, he turns toward me for the first time since we entered the car. His eyes blaze and his jaw is hard set, but the intensity he displays doesn't feel like anger, more an internal struggle of some kind.

"In case you're cold." He lays the suit coat over my exposed legs. When his fingers caress the skin on my upper thighs, I gasp, and he jumps like he touched a hot flame. "Pardon me."

"No worries." With shaky hands, I smooth his jacket over my legs. The soft wool feels warm from being wrapped around the larger-than-life man.

"The bakery owner assured me I bought the best cherry tart in Manhattan." I decide to try some small talk.

"Thanks for helping me out." Mr. Hammond looks at me with his intense dark eyes. My heart flutters as this beautiful man gives me his full attention. "We are on a mission to ensure he makes the Warwick Awards dinner this Saturday night. He's up for book of the year, and his attendance is uncertain."

"Why wouldn't he come?" I ask.

"That's the multi-million-dollar question. Literally." Mr. Hammond rakes his hands through his inky black hair, releasing a breath of frustration. "Since he's not answering our emails or calls, we're going to him. I'm banking on your fresh face versus my old mug getting us past the front door."

"I'll do my best not to fangirl too much. Where does he live?" I remember Mr. Black's bio mentioning New England and figure it can't be too far if we're driving there.

"In Greenwich, Connecticut. About an hour away." He shifts a bit closer to me, and our legs touch. He doesn't pull away, and our connection lingers, making my pulse race.

No man has ever had such an effect on me. I cross my legs and look out the front window for a few seconds, worried over what he'll see reflected in my eyes if I stay turned his way.

"Not far at all then." My voice trembles. *Does he notice?*

"I was raised in Greenwich too." He's sharing something personal with me, and I can't help feeling closer to this powerful man.

"I was raised in Alabama. Though, I'm sure that's not a surprise, considering how I talk."

"So was my mother. Your accent matches hers." My mouth flies open while the corners of his lips rise, turning into a full smile that makes me forget how to breathe. "Surprised, right?"

"Totally," I say in a weak voice.

I imagined his mother to be a refined socialite from the Upper East Side, educated at the finest prep schools where girls are polished to perfection. I wonder how she ended up in New York City and married to one of the most influential publishers in the city.

"She worked for the company after graduating from

Brown University." He either read my mind, or I asked my question out loud. The latter is likely.

"An office romance then," I say with a sneaky smile.

"Something like that." He straightens his already perfect tie. I do love watching his long fingers, though I wish he didn't skip over the juicy details.

Still, today, girls from Alabama rarely get accepted into Ivy League colleges. I can't imagine what it was like years ago when his mother went to school there.

"Your mother's smart," I blurt out.

"So are you." I wonder how he can say this about me based on our limited interaction. At least I'm not coming across as a country girl from the sticks.

"Thanks." My face blushes at his compliment, and he smiles back at me, only making my condition worse. I'm not used to having a man's attention aimed at me like this. It's all so overwhelming.

"Do you live in the city?" He finally asks me a personal question, but it still floats on the surface of small talk.

"Just visiting for a few days. By myself." I have no idea why I included my lone wolf status.

"I'm still unclear how you ended up in our lobby." He tilts his head and pauses. "But I appreciate your help today."

"I hope it works." Mr. Black's lack of cooperation is etched on Mr. Hammond's face, so I truly hope we can change his mind about this awards dinner. It sounds super important, especially if his book wins.

"Me too. Well, I need to make some calls while we're

driving," he says in a firm, deep voice, like he's switching from casual conversation to business mode.

"Of course." As CEO, nonstop calls and meetings have to fill his day. I can't expect him to entertain me the entire ride. Though I'd love to talk with him and get to know him better, I have to be realistic. He has a corporation to run.

Mr. Hammond stares at me for a few silent seconds, then drops his eyes to my mouth and follows a straight line down to my chest.

I squirm in my seat. He clears his throat and looks forward. This tension between us rises to a point where I might combust. I worry the windows will soon fog up, just like Maggie mentioned—and we haven't touched each other.

Dream on, Holly. The man is way out of my league.

He extends one leg and digs his phone out from his front pocket. I can't help but notice the fabric straining over his crotch, and there's something rather large outlined by his wool trousers.

Whoa.

I can't believe it. This hot, older man is turned on ... by *me*.

His insistence that I cover my exposed legs makes sense now. He wanted them out of *his* sight. It had nothing to do with me being cold. I gaze out the side window as the road flies by, a slow smile building across my face.

11

"Don't you agree, Mr. Hammond?" Mrs. Ratner, my human resource manager asks, but I have no clue what she wants me to agree on. All my calls have been a blur.

I run my fingers through my hair for the millionth time today. It has to be standing up on end by now. I blame my lack of concentration on the young woman sitting next to me with her shapely legs, long blond hair, and curves so dangerous, they should be illegal.

In fairness, it's not her fault she was born with everything that drives men wild. She actually comes across as more of an innocent, likely having no idea the effect she has on men —or me, for that matter.

Maybe it's her Alabama roots. My father often said southern women have a way of stealing a man's heart without him even knowing it. I believe he was speaking on his own personal experience since he married one. But when Miss Holly smiles up at me while playing with the strands of her hair and blinks her gorgeous blue eyes, there's a special magic she possesses aimed at me.

I don't remember ever being this distracted by a woman, even when my teenage hormones raged like wildfire. I'm a grown man and need to get my shit together. Too much is at stake for me to lose my bearings over a beautiful woman, especially one who's way too young for me.

I need to get laid.

I should take Lucas up on his offer, but who am I kidding? Some random pussy won't scratch this itch.

"Mr. Hammond, are you there?" Mrs. Ratner asks, her voice laced in concern. I never zone out with my staff. Ever.

"Could you repeat that last thing you were saying?"

"Of course," she says, graciously ignoring how out of it I am today. "We are still looking for a candidate to head millennial marketing. I feel we need to recruit someone who's already reaching this crowd. Like a blogger or social influencer."

"Sounds smart to me."

"What about the junior executive apartment?" she asks. "You mentioned it last week."

"Sure, if you find the right person, offer them the apartment at the subsidized discount. If it's a man, I sure hope he likes pink."

The apartment I bought for my former girlfriend is empty after our breakup, so I've turned it over for the company to use. No reason the place should gather dust. Besides, the housing costs in the city put many young people out of the market.

"Well, I have a résumé in hand that could be promising. It's a young woman whose blog appeals to twenty-some-things and beyond. Let's see how it goes."

"Keep me posted." We end the call just as the car pulls off the Merritt parkway in Connecticut. A quick glance out the window reveals the familiar winding, tree-lined streets of my hometown.

I glance over at Miss Holly. She types away on her phone, covering her mouth as she giggles. I smile at the sound and laugh quietly too. When she looks up at me with surprised eyes, it feels like she's been caught doing something wrong.

Was she?

I bet she's texting her boyfriend back in Alabama. A beauty like her can't be single. And if he had a brain in his head, he'd be here with her too. I wouldn't trust any man around her, including me.

"We're getting close," I say. She texts one more message, then turns off her phone, giving me her full attention. *Take that, boyfriend.*

She rises one hip off the seat a couple inches and stares

out the car window at the manicured mansions and estates with their long driveways. My suit coat slides down the tops of her smooth thighs. Her skin looks so soft and creamy. My fingers itch to touch her.

"Are those houses or lodges?" She peers over her shoulder, and tilts up one side of her mouth, catching me gazing at her thighs while I drown in my dirty thoughts.

"Homes," I rasp as the effect she has on me invades my voice.

"Wow. They're enormous." My childhood home looks similar and isn't too far from here. "When I see homes like this, I always wonder what the people do for a living."

"Most are top executives or business owners working in Manhattan. It's a bedroom community of commuters."

"Except Mr. Black," she mentions with a teasing smile.

"True. There's always the exception." I shake my head.

After a few more stops and turns, the car pulls up to Mr. Black's estate. In classic Connecticut style, a stonewall lines the property. The house sits far off the road, hidden from our view. My driver hesitates, stopping at the stately entrance.

"Go ahead, Lawrence," I direct. The car enters the property through the open gate, moving along a black paved driveway.

Mr. Black's estate comes into view, exploding over the rolling hill, and Miss Holly gasps. It contains ten bedrooms, and who the hell knows how many baths. I've been here one other time for Black's sixtieth surprise birthday party. He gave his wife hell about keeping the party a secret.

I hope this surprise visit doesn't tick him off too. Fortunately, I brought a gorgeous lucky charm with a cherry dessert. Her sweet southern accent and bright smile shouldn't hurt my cause either.

12

TESSA

I thought New York City was out of my element, but Mr. Black's house looks like something out of a Hollywood movie. It's larger than my entire high school back in Alabama.

"I can't believe that's his house." Mr. Hammond laughs, and I swat the air to hush him. "I pictured him living in a log cabin somewhere in the woods of New England, typing away on his laptop. Not this."

"It's actually his wife's family estate. But you didn't hear that from me." Mr. Hammond buttons his lips with a twist of his fingers.

The driver eases the car up to the front circle drive. A large wood and iron front door sits in the middle of the monstrosity. It looks more like the entrance to a castle, where one would find Elizabeth Bennett and Mr. Darcy. I'm surprised a line of servants isn't greeting us. Maybe it's because we are in stealth mode.

When the car stops, there's a fluttering in the pit of my stomach. It's not every day a person gets to meet their literary hero. I wring my hands and smooth my hair, resisting the urge to twirl it between my fingers. Old habits die hard.

"Nervous?" Mr. Hammond asks, glancing at my hands.

"Just a little bit." The car stops, and I hold my stomach. I feel like throwing up. Maybe it's the early morning mimosa. Bad decision. "What if I say something stupid? Like, I've read all your books and love them? I have to be more creative."

"He's going to love you."

"I'm not so sure. Look at me."

"Believe me, I can't stop." The wicked tease in his eyes quickens my pulse and lightens the mood. So what if I look like a midday stripper delivering a "special" message under my coat.

I hand Mr. Hammond's jacket back to him and try to pull the hem of my coat down. Nothing helps, so I give up.

The driver opens the car door for me, and I take the bag containing the cherry tart from him. Mr. Hammond puts his jacket back on, and it falls in place without him having to straighten it. He walks around to my side of the car and places his hand on my lower back to guide me forward.

He moves his thumb in small circles just above my waist-line. Shivers follow. He stills his finger for a split second, then resumes his movements. I don't look up at him fearing I'll falter. It's all too much.

We walk side by side toward the front door, but I stop a few feet from it. Yesterday, I was walking the rich soils of Alabama, and now I stand in front of my favorite author's mansion. *What is this life?* When my eyes meet Mr. Hammond's, his handsome face twists in worry. I guess my fears are broadcast all over my face.

"You ready?" He moves a hair from my cheek, and I savor his tenderness. The gentle touch works to calm my fears. I can do this. For *him.*

Next to the large door, an intercom panel glows from blue lights underneath numerous buttons. The largest one has writing over it, saying: Door bell, obviously.

"I can guess who wrote that." Mr. Hammond moves to push the bell, announcing our arrival. I shift from side to side, gripping the bakery bag in my hands.

A long minute goes by, but no one comes to answer the door.

"Do you think he's not home?" I ask.

"It's a possibility. Do you like cherry tarts?" Mr. Hammond's smile doesn't reach his eyes.

"Don't tell Mr. Black this, but I'm not a fan of cherries.

I'm wild about strawberries, though. My grandparents have a dairy farm back in Alabama and grew—"

Before I finish, the iron handle clicks, silencing me on the spot. I glance up at Mr. Hammond as the door begins to creak open. He's leaning forward. I'm holding my breath.

As the hinges continue to moan, Mr. Black appears before us in a gray sweater, matching his thick hair, and black pressed trousers. He's shoeless with bright white socks covering his feet. I swallow a giggle.

His reading spectacles rest at the end of his nose as he narrows his eyes looking between Mr. Hammond and me. Deep lines scatter across his forehead. Mr. Black doesn't seem amused. Quite the opposite, judging by his marked scowl.

"Barclay," Mr. Black says in an abrasive tone. It's not a good sound, especially since we're trying to break the ice and get on his good side.

"Don. This is Tessa Holly." Mr. Hammond gestures toward me. I crack a small grin at Mr. Black, but his face is frozen in a frown.

When no one moves or speaks for a few seconds, the air thickens with tension. I feel words bubbling up inside me and try to contain them, but it's no use. I hate awkward moments more than missing a sale on my favorite skinny jeans. Besides, Mr. Hammond brought me along for a purpose, so I might as well get to it.

"We brought you a cherry tart," I announce, walking

forward a couple steps while extending the bag out in front of me. Mr. Black focuses on the bag, then drops down to my legs. One corner of his mouth tips up as he meets my eyes. His frown has disappeared. *Bingo.* I can work with this.

I remove the tart from the bag and flip open the lid. The sweet aroma fills the space around us, drawing Mr. Black to the edge of the doorway like a magnet. He takes the box in his hands and brings it up to his nose. Closing his eyes, he takes a deep breath.

"This smells divine," Mr. Black says in blissful approval. I smile up at Mr. Hammond, and when he gleams back at me, I melt.

"The bakery claims it's the best in Manhattan, and I thought you'd like to give it a try."

Luckily, Mr. Hammond takes over the conversation. I'm still worried I'll blurt out some fangirl nonsense. I feel the words, "I'm your biggest fan," dancing on the tip of my tongue. God help me.

"So, you just happened to be in the neighborhood, or were you on the way to your family home around the corner?" Mr. Black grips the boxed tart, pulling it closer to himself. At least we scored on the dessert.

I stand wide-eyed realizing Mr. Hammond was raised in a home like this estate with servants and silver spoons. I shrink inside, feeling like the complete outsider between these two wealthy men.

"Hell, Don, you know exactly why I'm here," Mr. Hammond scoffs, pushing his hands into his pant pockets.

"Yeah. Yeah," Mr. Black mutters, backing away from the entrance. "Might as well come inside. I'll give you fifteen minutes. After that, I'm eating my tart."

Mr. Black grins at me with a devilish flash in his eyes. I knew I'd love him.

13

BARCLAY

Miss Holly and I cross the threshold, following Don inside. Classical tapestries hug the walls of the entryway, along with several large cats. My nose twitches. I try not to recoil when a fluffy gray one approaches me, weaving through my legs, pressing against my slacks. The guards at Buckingham Palace don't stand as still as me. Thankfully, Miss Holly bends down, reaching out a hand toward the furry creature.

"What a sweetie pie," she purrs as the cat moves toward her. She tickles her fingers under the cat's chin. "What's its name?"

"That's Darcy," Don says. Another cat saunters over to

greet Miss Holly. I might end up needing an epi-pen before I leave this house. "Along with his companion, Elizabeth."

"Literary names. I love it." Miss Holly stands up, and it's a damn good thing too. I caught a glimpse of white lace peeking out from under the edge of her short hem. I'm facing death by dander and trench coat.

"My wife, Gertrude, keeps adopting these four-footed animals. After all, Saint Gertrude is the patron saint of cats, though she does let me name them. Catsby's over in the corner." Don points to a sleek black feline sprawled near a marble statue of Venus. Figures he's seated at the foot of a love goddess.

I sneeze a couple times. *Shit.* My neck feels itchy too. Wonder if we can take the meeting outside ...

"You okay, Barclay?" Don asks.

"Allergies," I cough out between sneezes. Where were all the cats during his sixtieth birthday party?

"You need some fresh air. Let's talk out on the veranda," Don says, then turns to Miss Holly. "Do you work for Hammond Press?"

"I do not," she says, looking at me to fill in the blanks.

What are they really? Who is she? That's the better question.

The hot girl I saw last night shows up in my office, wears a trench coat while her clothes are cleaned, and I'm using her to get you to open the door. Yeah, that doesn't sound professional, or believable given she looks like a strip-a-gram.

"We're friends. She's visiting from Alabama."

"Oh." Don darts his eyes between us. "Family friends then?"

"Something like that," I say before I can even think. *What's wrong with me?* I never lie. I'll blame it on my brain fog from the cats and virginal panties.

Don squints one eye and shakes his head. One glance at Miss Holly's shocked expression makes me wonder if he knows the truth.

"Tessa. It's all right if I call you that, since you're Barclay's friend?"

"Of course. I'm not used to being this formal around *friends*." She looks at me, eyes full of mischief.

"Would you mind entertaining yourself in my library while Barclay and I talk business?"

"Your library? Really?" she asks with eager surprise as Don nods. "I can't believe it."

"It's the second room on the right." Don gives her a warm smile and leads us down a hallway with an arched entrance. He opens a large wooden door, and we enter into the library. "Help yourself with anything on the shelves. My library is yours."

Bookcases line the side walls, while the back one has floor-to-ceiling windows, letting light pour into the library. The sun catches Miss Holly's golden hair, making an angelic halo, and I can't look away from her. Her beauty leaves me breathless—or it's the felines.

"It's beautiful. Thanks," she says in a dreamy voice.

Holding her hands to her chest, she walks toward Don

and stops in front of him. She reaches up on her tiptoes to give him a quick kiss on his cheek. Pleased with himself, and her, he smirks. I ball my fist.

"You're welcome," he sputters. *Southern women.*

He bends down to pick up a small kitten standing near his feet. The cat's fur is a butterscotch color. Calico, I think, and a damn cute one too. "I've named this little guy Shakespurr after a new blog I found. Have you heard of it?"

Don looks at me for an answer, but I have no clue. I shift on my feet when Miss Holly pipes up, hopefully saving the day again.

"I know that blog," she gushes with excitement.

"My agent turned me on to it. It's not every day a millennial crowd get books written by an old man like me."

"That's not true. Believe me. I'm one of your biggest fans," she exclaims, then proceeds to turn bright red and bows her head. "I swore I wouldn't say that."

When her shoulders fall, I want to tell her not to worry, because he hears that all the time, but that's likely the very reason she's embarrassed. It's what everyone says to him.

"What was your favorite book?" Don asks, a big grin on his face, eating up this beautiful young woman's attention. *Where's his wife anyway?*

"*His Secret* was your best thriller, in my opinion." Miss Holly gives him a dazzling smile. "You're the king of writing palpable tension. Never letting the reader know how you plan on peeling the onion."

"Wow." Don whistles, and I stand amazed at Miss Holly's

assessment. She's nailed his unique brand. It keeps the pages turning and the books selling. "You truly are familiar with the Shakespurr blog. It's almost exactly what they said about the book."

"Uh-huh," she singsongs, tilting her lips in a smile of victory. She should be proud she cracked this stubborn man's crusty exterior.

"Follow me to the kitchen, Barclay. You need meds before your lips take over your entire face." Don crooks a finger over his shoulder as he walks toward the library door.

"Great," I grunt.

I touch my lips. Damn fluffy fur flying in the air. One cat makes me sneeze and scratch, but apparently a house full of felines requires major drugs.

"Behave," I whisper to Miss Holly before I follow behind Don.

She bites her lip, and damn if I don't want to kiss the living breath out of her. Aside from her not being an employee, it's best we are separated during my talk with Don. Everything about her distracts me to no end.

Once in the kitchen, Don turns on his oven and places his tart inside it. He gives me a glass of water, along with a Claritin. I swallow back the pill, hoping the medicine works quickly. I need to be sharp with so much at stake today.

Don shows the way to his large veranda, and I swear this house needs a map to navigate the rooms. Once outside, we look over a sculptured garden where a glimmering pool shines in the late morning sun. Thankfully, I don't see a cat in sight.

"Gertrude likes to open the pool the first of May, though the water feels like the Artic until late July." Don guides me to a large wrought iron table with cushioned chairs. "Please, sit."

We both take a seat, and I set my glass of water down on the table. Clearing my throat, I begin.

"Don, we need you at the Warwick Awards Saturday night." I hold nothing back. After all, he's only giving me fifteen minutes. "Why haven't you answered a single email or call from us?"

"I was waiting," he says, picking a piece of invisible lint from his pants.

"For what?" His answer perplexes me. I can't read minds. "Is Mort offering you more?" I adjust my collar.

"Hell, he's always offering me more, but that's not the reason I haven't responded." Don takes a breath before continuing, and I find myself on the edge of my seat—and possibly my career. "I was waiting for you to reach out to me."

"Me?" It makes no sense. "Fill me in."

"Well, your father was my go-between at Hammond Press, and I was expecting the same thing from you after he left. Instead, I was shuffled off to an editor."

"I had no idea you were such a diva." I laugh, and Don smiles. "So that's it? If I work with you, you'll come Saturday night?"

"Believe me. I was going to show up. Though, I wasn't sure which table I would sit at. Mort happened to mention he had an empty chair."

My jaw tightens at the thought of Don at Mort's table. Mort's mocking smile flies through my mind, though I imagine his yellowing teeth.

"I bet he did," I retort. "I'll let my editor know you're straight lined to me moving forward."

"I was giving you until tomorrow. By the way, the cherry tart was a nice touch. Not to mention, the gorgeous delivery girl ... or 'friend.'" He chuckles, using air quotes.

"We're just friends." I try to define the lie I spoke only minutes ago. It's more a hope than a deception, because I would like to be her friend while she's in New York City. Return the favor preferably with her in my arms.

"I don't understand this 'friends' business with young people. Men didn't nuance their relationships with women in my day."

"It's not like that," I object, because random hookups have never been part of my sex life. However, I can't say how many girlfriends I've had over the years. Dozens perhaps.

"Sure," he says with an epic eye-roll. "She's smart and beautiful." He pauses a beat. "You're stupid."

"She's too young."

It's a fact—not an excuse. I've never dated anyone more than four years younger than me.

"That's not what your father thought when he met your

mother. He also never called her his friend." Don crosses his arms over his chest, a look of victory in his eyes.

"But he did call her his secretary," I say with a smirk, knowing my mother was so much more than an office worker to my father. She was, and still is, his everything.

"Minor details," Don says in a matter-of-fact tone, and we both smile, because he's right. Age is just a number when two adults are attracted to each other, or so I've heard from my parents.

"The devil is usually in those pesky details," I add.

I hardly know anything about Miss Holly, other than she's from Alabama, and maybe a little too trusting if she came to help me today without any solid facts.

"As you get older, you learn the devil haunts your regrets." Don stays stone-faced, and I let his words of wisdom sink in. "Bring Tessa to the awards dinner. Make an old man happy and sit her next to me. In the meantime, I hope you get your head out of your ass and realize you can't be friends with a woman like her. I can tell she's already gotten under your skin."

Has she? Or do I just want to get under her trench coat?

14

TESSA

I run my fingers along a shelf in Don's library. I can't believe he and I are on a first name basis. I want to call my mother, the true lover of books, and tell her what's happened today. Everything seems so surreal, I wonder if she'd even believe me.

I spot one of my favorite books, *The Count of Monte Cristo*, and pull it from a tightly packed shelf. The leather edition is worn around the edges and the gold embossed writing on the surface has faded with time. I let the large book fall open in my hands, revealing a page with a crushed dried rose. I hold the delicate flower in place, wondering if Don left the faded red rose inside years ago.

Before I close the book, I notice a passage marked with hearts in the side margin. *"Woman is sacred; the woman one loves is holy."*

I want to believe Don highlighted these words and saved the rose in remembrance of the woman he loves or loved. He does weave a thread of romance throughout his stories, as so many great authors tend to do. I've always thought the greatest books would be mere words on a page without a lovers' struggle within them.

Carefully, I close the book and return it to its rightful place. I glance over the shelves, searching for another title amongst the hundreds. As I reach for *The Sound and the Fury* by fellow southerner, Tennessee Williams, my phone vibrates, alerting me to an incoming text.

I reach into my coat pocket and pull it out. After a quick glance at the screen, it shows I've missed five texts from Maggie. The last one begs me to call her, so I do. She answers after the first ring.

"So, spill." The words fly out without even a quick hello. Talk about anxious for details.

"We're at Don Black's house—or more like his mansion. I've never seen a home like this before." I move over to a lush velvet couch and sit down. I choose a seat that gives me a full view of the library's door. If Don wasn't kidding, he's only giving Mr. Hammond fifteen minutes, so I'll be ready in case their meeting ends soon.

"Is your head spinning?" Maggie asks.

"You have no idea. But there's something wrong with me," I confess, twirling a strand of hair around my finger.

"What could possibly be wrong? You're with a hot as fuck guy in your favorite author's home. You're living your best life."

"True, but I keep picturing Mr. Hammond with his clothes off. Who does that?" My face falls, causing my hair to cascade around me.

"Finally. It's happened," Maggie yells with glee, piercing my ear. "Don't worry. I do that all the time when I'm attracted to a hot guy. I've gotten so good at imagining what's behind their zippers, I wonder if I don't have X-ray vision or something."

"But we're talking about me. Virgin Tessa here." I've never tried to picture what a man has in his pants until today.

When I feel a prickle of awareness against my skin, like someone's watching me, I quickly lift my head and blink.

Mr. Hammond leans against the door, his arms over his chest. His impassive stare gives nothing away, but his steady position tells me one thing: he's been standing there long enough to hear what I said to Maggie.

I want to die or spontaneously combust.

"Oh, shit. He's here," I whisper into the phone, then end the call without waiting for her response. She's probably laughing her ass off at my expense while I consider jumping out a window.

Since Mr. Hammond takes up the entire doorway, and also the only exit for the library, there's only thing I can do to save my dignity: pretend the conversation with Maggie never happened. Maybe he'll be a gentleman and pretend right along with me.

"Ready to leave?" Mr. Hammond pushes off the doorframe and slips his hands into his pockets. I can't tell whether he heard my naughty confession, along with my sexual status. He's an ace at the poker face.

I rise to my feet and straighten my trench coat in hopes of making it cover more of my skin. I feel so exposed under his watchful eye, it unnerves me.

"Ready," I answer. He assesses me from head to toes as I walk toward him. My feet are unsteady once I'm by his side.

"Who were you speaking with?" he asks, tilting his head.

"That conversation wasn't meant for your ears." My face flushes, and saving my dignity seems impossible at this point.

I can't even look up at him now, so I walk past him into the hallway. I hear his shoes hitting the marble floor right behind me, and I continue to the foyer, looking for Don.

"Okay, it was rude of me to eavesdrop," he admits. Shocked, I turn to gauge the look in his eyes. Is he truly sorry?

He looks at me with a touch of irritation, and his jaw remains tight. Definitely not the soothing expression one would hope to find from a contrite confessor.

"Do you realize how embarrassing this is to me? I thought you were a gentleman, Mr. Hammond," I scold, my hands planted on my hips.

"A gentleman? Tessa, there's no such thing in Manhattan." He squints his eyes at me in warning, and I want to slap him across the face. I refrain, of course, mostly because I couldn't reach his cheeks without a stepstool.

Why do I feel this anger toward him? Maybe I want to see him without his clothes on after all. And now that he knows I've never slept with anyone, a man of his experience will never want me.

I hear a chuckling behind me, and spin around to see Don. He shakes his head while looking between Mr. Hammond and me.

"Looks like I interrupted a lover's quarrel from the expressions on your faces," Don says with a knowing smile.

"Miss Holly—" Mr. Hammond starts to speak.

"You mean Tessa. After all, she does hate being so formal with friends," Don corrects, smirking at me. I truly love this wonderful man's sense of humor. Somehow, he gets me.

"Yes," Mr. Hammond huffs while running his fingers through his thick black hair. "Tessa and I need to get back to Manhattan."

"Don't want to keep the big city waiting." Don waves his hands toward the front door, practically shooing us out of his house. "It'll just leave more of the cherry tart for me. I hate to share anyway."

"I'll see you Saturday night," Mr. Hammond says as he opens the front door.

"Yes. I'll be there. And, Tessa, I hope to see you again real soon," he says with a crooked smile, while Mr. Hammond clenches his perfect jaw.

"Me too," I reply.

The next thing I know, Mr. Hammond has his hand on the small of my back and ushers—*pushes*—me out of Don's house. He leads me toward the black town car where his driver sits behind the wheel, or more like sleeps, guessing by the angle of his head.

"Be a good girl and get in the backseat," Mr. Hammond demands after his driver opens the passenger door for me, but my feet stay planted on the paved driveway. I'll be a bad girl until I clear up one thing.

"You heard what I said to my friend, didn't you, Barclay?" Calling him by his first name feels right, especially since we're discussing my sex life, or lack thereof.

"Yes, Tessa. I heard it all," he confesses, distress in his voice. He takes a deep breath and rubs the back of his neck. His dark eyes gaze down at me with unreadable emotions swirling in them. I wish I knew what he's thinking. "Get in the car."

Great. This should be a fun ride back to the city.

15

BARCLAY

After Tessa finally gets into the car, I round the trunk and lean against the door I should be opening, but I can't just yet. I take a few deep breaths, because I need time to process one monumental fact: she's a *virgin*. The word burns into my brain. My mind spins a million different scenarios knowing she wants me naked and has never slept with anyone.

And how's my traitorous body reacting to both realties? I'm as hard as the granite stone driveway under my feet.

If I use the head on top of my shoulders, which is usually the case when it comes to women, I'll ask Lawrence to drive her back to the city, alone, without me. Then I'll order an

Uber or walk to the train station a couple miles away to let off some steam.

I pace beside the car, rubbing the back of my neck. I need to stay away from her at all costs. The idea of us together isn't just about age anymore. Hell, I've never been with a virgin, even back in my school days. She needs someone who can commit to her beyond one night or a few days while she's here in the city.

She's the kind of girl a guy brings home to meet his mother, and mine would love her too. There's no way I can fuck a virgin—and that's all it would be.

Even after admitting I'm definitely not that man for her, I find myself grabbing the door handle and getting in the damn car. I'm thinking with the wrong part of my body. In one quick move I'm sitting next to her in the backseat, my eyes trained ahead of me, but I see her in my periphery. Golden hair and creamy long legs pop against the black leather interior. A man would have to be blind to miss her.

"Lawrence, we're ready to head back to the office." I fix my seatbelt and straighten my jacket. They're simple memory movements that should settle my rapid pulse and distract me from Tessa—and her virginity and desire to see me naked—but my heart keeps pounding away.

"Yes, Mr. Hammond." My driver starts the car and eases it down the long driveway. I want to yell at him to press the gas pedal and get this vehicle moving. Instead, I tap a finger rhythmically against my thigh.

All my senses are on high alert in the tight confines of the car. I lean back against the leather headrest, making a futile attempt to handle the proximity of the blonde bombshell next to me.

I'm trapped as her fragrant perfume floats around me like a siren's song. I fight the crazy urge to pull her closer and inhale her scent. I crave the feel of her soft and delicate thighs. I'm drowning in her presence, yet I don't take off my jacket to cover her legs. I want to feast on them one last time, even if it's pure torture.

I try to convince myself I'm protecting her, but is that true? Or could I be guarding myself from her? It would take nothing for me to get lost in the curves of her body and never come up for air.

I close my eyes and imagine her legs wrapped around me. Our lips pressed together. Tongues. Hell, I better stop this train of thought, because I have no will power concerning her. All she has to do is ask, and I'd be hers.

"Barclay," she whispers, breaking our game of silence. I jerk when she touches my fisted hand resting on the leather seat between us. "It's really okay if I call you that now?"

"Sure, Tessa. You're not my employee."

When I turn toward her and our eyes lock, she steals my breath away. Her big baby blues beg for me to let her in, like she's searching for the smallest fissure in my heart. But I can only stay on the surface with her. Anything else will remove the last bit of control I possess.

"Then we can start over and be friends?" she asks. Her

voice is tender and seeking. "Pretend you didn't hear every-thing. I'm humiliated beyond belief."

She doesn't deny what she said, but Don warned me it was impossible for me to be her friend. I'll prove him wrong. I can handle a friendly conversation for an hour-long drive back to the office. It's a piece of cake, though bringing her Saturday night to the dinner is completely out of the question.

Her alluring mix of innocence and beauty requires one thing: I have to go cold turkey. From here on out, this will have to be our last and final contact. Otherwise, she might not stay a virgin very long.

"What conversation?" I wink at her, and she turns a pretty shade of pink.

I unfurl my fingers, and she removes her light touch. "Tell me about yourself."

When she beams up at me all dewy-eyed and eager, a part of me already misses seeing her smile. I scan her face, capturing the moment and labeling her as the one who got away or I let go before it started. It's for the best, though. I feel like a panting wolf wanting to devour a trusting lamb.

"Okay." She perks up in her seat. Her bright eyes are aglow with my fixed attention. "I grew up in Monroeville, Alabama. I'm sure you've never heard of it."

"I'd have to trade in my publishing credentials if I didn't know the hometown of Truman Capote and Harper Lee. Besides, my mother was raised in Birmingham."

"It practically makes us family friends," she laughs, and it sounds so youthful and sweet, reminding me again of our age difference. Then her laughter fades, along with her smile. "I'm curious. Why did you lie to Don about us?"

"I have no clue." I run a hand over my face, trying to make the awkward moment disappear. I opt for changing the subject. "By the way, everything's okay with him now. I want to thank you for your help."

"That's great. The tart worked then?"

"I'd say it was more you giving it to him. He was quite impressed with your review of his book. So was I. You know you never really told me what you're doing in New York City."

"I just graduated college and ..." She hesitates before continuing, twisting a lock of hair. She bites down on her bottom lip, like she's trying not to say something. "And ... well, I'm here for a few days looking for a job."

"Bright lights, big city," I answer, and she nods.

My first thought is: do we have a job for her at Hammond Press? Then I realize how impossible it would be having her working there. She'd be too close and tempting.

"Exactly. I've always wanted to live here, so does my best friend. If I find a position, she's moving here too." Her brow wrinkles slightly, her eyes expressing concern. "Well, I can't let her down."

"Good luck. I'm sure you'll find something," I say.

My words contain very little enthusiasm, and I feel like a complete asshole. All I'd have to do is call my HR head, and she'd wave a magic wand for Tessa, finding her a suitable job at the company. She does seem to love books. And we all need to start somewhere. My fingers itch to grab my phone, but I keep them resting at my side.

"I have six more days to figure it out. That's plenty of time, right?" She worries her lip, and I feel even shittier for doing nothing to help this sweet young woman. Dammit. I have to do something.

"Give me your phone." I hold out my open palm. She places her cell phone in my hand without a single question. Her trust should make me feel better, but it has the opposite effect, since I don't deserve it.

I click her phone to light up the screen, and it displays a tall handsome man with his arm around her. "Boyfriend?"

"It's my older brother. There's no boyfriend," she utters, and I try to contain a smile while entering my phone number into her cell and texting myself.

The guys in Alabama are complete idiots. Then again, if she had a boyfriend, my worries would be over, because I'd have the best reason to stay away from her. She could never be mine. What's troubling, though, is I'm way too happy to find out she's single.

I hand the phone back to her and pick up mine. "Text me your email. I'll forward the names of a couple people looking for interns at their companies. You can drop my name, tell them I gave you their information, if you'd like."

I don't know enough about her to really be a good reference, but I'll take a gamble and consider it payback for helping me out with Don today.

"I can't tell you how much I appreciate this," she gushes, moving closer to me, then gently squeezes my hand. "Thanks so much."

She needs to quit touching me. I'm reaching the threshold of my control here.

"You're welcome, though I can't guarantee anything." I remove my hand before I wrap it around her small one.

Needing a distraction from everything Tessa, I check my phone to see who needs something from me, because there's always someone wanting my assistance or an answer. I can't remember the last time I fell off the office grid like this during a workday.

I scroll through several emails that can wait for my response until later, then I see a text from Mrs. Mackenzie wanting to know where to send Tessa's dry-cleaned clothes. She's asking for her address.

Finding out where Tessa's staying in the city isn't smart, especially since I'm resolved to go cold turkey once she's out of this car. But she does need her clothes back.

I turn toward Tessa in search of the answers Mrs. Mackenzie needs, and get sidetracked by her shapely legs. I caress them with a slow gaze, then follow a curvy trail up to her eyes, imagining her without a stitch on. This time, I'm the one with the dirty thoughts.

16

TESSA

The way Barclay looks at me leaves me breathless and tied in knots. My skin feels so on fire under his gaze, I want to unbutton my coat and let out some steam. But I only have on my bra and panties, so I spread the collar open wider in hopes of getting a little air on my overheated skin. Nothing helps.

Barclay swallows. "Where are you staying in the city?" His eyes search mine.

"The Hammond Hotel. Room six-seventeen," I breathe. He frowns, and I have no idea why.

"Lawrence," Barclay calls out in a firm voice. "We need to drop Miss Holly off at the Hammond first, then my office."

"Yes, sir," Lawrence replies, facing forward, his hands gripped firm on the steering wheel.

"Mrs. Mackenzie will send your clothes to your hotel room. You can leave her coat at the front desk."

Like he's checked off a task from a list, Barclay returns back to his phone and types away on the screen. And me? Well, I try to process why he just called me Miss Holly. Maybe it's because he's speaking to his driver.

Either way, I can' help but worry and feel restless the closer we get to Manhattan. There's no guarantee I'll see Barclay again once I exit this car.

My unease started back at Don's when Barclay hesitated to get in the car with me. He walked by the passenger door several times, worry lines crossing his forehead and creasing at his eyes. He seemed at war with something.

It doesn't take a membership to Mensa to know what it is either. My virginal status spooks him. His reaction is nothing new to me.

Guys either run for the hills when they find out, or pursue me as a selfish challenge, hoping they can add a special notch to their bedpost.

I've yet to find a guy who sticks around for the right reason, or one I'd even consider the right one for me—until yesterday. One look from Barclay Hammond across the restaurant, and my body was turned on without even a touch. I was a smoldering mess last night. Today, I'm more of a hot mess, which leads me to the impossibilities of us being together.

He's the kind of guy who deserves his own lifestyle spread in GQ magazine. I can see the caption for his story. *Meet Barclay Hammond, New York City's Most Eligible Bachelor.* They'd ask him questions about what he's looking for in a woman. He'd say something like beautiful, accomplished, and experienced. She'd have to be someone worthy of his sophistication.

Why would he want me, some virgin college graduate, when he could have any woman in his bed? Being around him has made me hope for the impossible. It's time to virgin up and forget my silly fantasies. He and I just aren't going to happen.

I glance over at him, and he's still on his phone, conquering the publishing world. I let out a long sigh and lean against the door. Gazing out my window, I watch the Manhattan skyline move closer. My time with him is almost up.

Who knows how many silent minutes later, Lawrence enters the busy streets of the city, and a lump forms in my throat. I want to say something to Barclay, like, *"What are you doing for the rest of your day? Any more authors you need help with?"* but I don't want to interrupt him. His brow creases in concentration, so whatever he's working on must be important.

"Check your phone," he says in his usual bossy tone. I turn from the window and find him assessing me with his dark eyes.

I do as he asks, and there are several unread texts from a

phone number with a New York City area code. It has to be him.

I open up the first text and glance over it. He's sent me the name and email address of a human resources manager. They also work for a company on my list of potential dream employers, but the address is different than the general one I've sent scores of emails to. I view all the other texts, and they're all similar. He's been working on his phone this entire time to help me find a job, and here I thought he was just ignoring me.

I smile up at him in sheer disbelief, and he returns mine with a sweet smirk, like it was nothing, but I know better. He's giving me access to people who trust him, without a clue as to whether I would be hirable or not. I owe him big time.

"I can't believe you did this for me," I say, nearly in tears. I'll blame it on that stupid lump in my throat.

I click my seatbelt off, throw it to the side, and move closer to him. Our legs touch, and I reach up to kiss him. When my lips meet his scruffy cheeks for a quick peck, he gasps and goes still.

Oh no, I've overstepped some boundary.

As quick as possible, I scoot back over to my side of the backseat. He resumes breathing, and our eyes meet. His are as black as night.

"I'm happy to help you, Tessa," he says in a husky voice. His intense gaze startles me, because I can't tell if he's mad or ready to pounce. My needy body hopes for the latter.

"Sir, we're here," his driver announces. The car comes to a stop outside Hammond Hotel, and the tension building between us dissipates.

Barclay lowers his head and pushes a breath out between his lips. It sounds like a long sigh of relief, likely since I'm getting out of the car. I fear my kiss was probably over the top. I hope he doesn't regret helping me.

"I'll get her door, Lawrence," he says, already halfway out of the vehicle. He has my door open in a flash, his hand extended. I place my shaky one in his and exit the car with his help.

Still clasping hands and standing on the sidewalk, I squint up at him, trying to block the midday sun. He's beautiful from my vantage point almost a foot below him. His hard jaw is framed with perfect scruff. His black eyes shine with vigor and strength, but there's a hint of something else behind them. Determination, maybe.

I'll never meet a more gorgeous man. It can't be humanly possible. I memorize his face, the touch of his hand holding mine, the way his eyes regard me. My heart aches, because, in this moment, I know it's our goodbye. Tears start to fill my eyes, and I pray he says something, anything. Finally, he does.

"Tessa." My name rolls off his tongue in a slow, reverent way. He doesn't seem mad, relieving some of my fears. I still believe he's dismissing me. Though his voice and eyes may say differently, his guarded stance is clearly telling me goodbye. "Thanks again for all your help today."

He lifts my hand to his mouth and grazes my knuckles with his lips. My knees almost give way. I feel his soft touch in hidden places that ache for him. If only he'd let me in. He blinks and drops my hand, then a second later, his eyes blaze anew at me, making me wonder what he truly feels.

"On the way back to the city, I emailed the manager at the hotel," he says, tossing his head back toward the building behind him. "I told him to comp all your meals, even your hotel minibar while you're here."

"You don't need to do all that, really. It's too much," I stammer on, confused by all his goodness, yet odd aloofness. *What am I missing?* "You've done more than enough by giving me all the contacts, plus I got to meet my favorite author. I'm still pinching myself."

"Good luck, Tessa," he says, straightening his perfect tie. His eyes shutter to a cooler version of himself. The heat is gone. I bite my lip as tears threaten again. "I hope you find what you're looking for."

"You too, Barclay," I whisper. His head tilts, and for a brief second, I think he's going to say something to me. Instead, he turns and walks back to his car.

I stand alone on the sidewalk with a hand at my throat and watch him pull away. I wave at him like a lovesick teenager, but he doesn't turn around in his seat. Probably for the best.

I walk through the buzzing lobby of my hotel. Happy people and smiling faces surround me, eager to see what this city has to offer. I feel as if the best thing about Manhattan just drove away.

Exhausted from the day's roller coaster of emotions, I drag my feet down the hallway to my room. When I place the keycard over the lock, a green light glows, and I turn the door handle. Once inside my room, I notice a red-foil balloon shaped like a strawberry floating in the air. A long yellow ribbon connects it to a platter of chocolate-covered strawberries sitting on the desk.

"Barclay?" I ask in the quietest whisper. My chin trembles. He remembered.

Instead of walking over to the desk and opening the card lying next to the strawberries, I collapse onto the crisp covers of the bed and let go of the tears I've been holding at bay, releasing the tightness in my throat. I curl into a ball and sob.

I'll feel better once I cry this man out of my system. The problem is, I don't want his help or gifts, though I appreciate all he's done. What I truly want is him.

17

"Sir. It's after seven." Mrs. Mackenzie stands at my office door, wearing the same trench coat that hugged Tessa's curves twenty-four hours ago. The cleaners returned it this afternoon, pressed and bagged. It seems Tessa was an apparition, appearing in my life to haunt me.

"Enjoy your weekend. I'll see you Monday," I say, eyeing her over my computer screen. She flings the long strap of her purse over a shoulder, but doesn't leave. There must be unfinished business. "Anything else?"

"I wanted to follow up on the awards dinner. They've asked the name of your plus one." She waits for my reply, tapping a sensible heel on the marble floor.

I want to say it's none of their damn business, but only because I haven't secured a date yet. Tessa's the one woman I'd like to bring, but happens to be the last woman I should take.

Cold turkey, I keep silently chanting, but I'm not convincing myself. I've opened my phone and glanced at her saved number a hundred times since I left her on the sidewalk yesterday. I almost had Lawrence circle the car back around to the hotel. Driving away from her and ignoring the powerful connection between us was one of the hardest things I've done in my life. I still regret it, but what choice did I have? Our timing is off by at least ten years.

A part of me hoped to hear from her today too, acknowledging that she'd received the chocolate-covered strawberries I had placed in her room. But she's been silent. It's for the best.

"Tell the event coordinator you weren't able to confirm the name." Mrs. Mackenzie tilts her head, giving me a puzzled look. "Do you have a problem with that?"

"No, sir." She sighs, shaking her head and rolling her eyes. "You did get the message from Mr. Black requesting Tessa Holly sits next him?" The slightest smile moves across her face.

"I did," I say, matter-of-fact, giving nothing away. "That nosy man needs to mind his own business."

"Good luck telling him that." She laughs at my expense, straightening her coat belt, just like Tessa did the day before. "Good night, Mr. Hammond."

After Mrs. Mackenzie leaves, I scan the weekly sales figures. When the numbers blur before me, I give up for the night and shut down my computer. Preparing to leave, I grab my phone off the desk and stare at the black screen. Ignoring the voice of reason, I pull up her number and pound out a text. My finger hovers over the send button, but then I remember her cloudy blue eyes calling to me as I walked away and push send.

Did you like the strawberries?

I stare at the screen and wait. A minute passes, then another, until finally, it displays the bubbling dots of a possible incoming text. I hold my breath like a desperate sixteen-year-old schoolboy. Even my hands start perspiring.

Yes. They were very juicy.

Jesus. My mind flies into overdrive. I imagine her biting into the chocolate layer with the fruit beneath. Juice spills over her full pink lips, running down her chin. My mouth starts to water, and not for the strawberry—for her. Kill me now.

I should just let it go, let *her* go, but I can't. It does feel safer just texting. It's not like I'm actually going to see her again. It's completely harmless.

What are you up to?

At least I didn't ask what she's wearing, though I'd love to know.

Getting ready for a drink date.

Date? The word slaps me across the face, and the floor

drops out from under me. *Who the hell is she going out with?* I fear it's some wolf wandering the streets looking for an innocent young woman to devour. It's how I felt about her, but I stepped away, controlled myself.

I want to ask who she's seeing, find out all the details, but I'm too late. I should've never left her alone.

"Dammit." My voice fills the empty office. I scrub a hand over my face, frustrated and unsure how to respond … if at all. I decide not to text her back. Why torture myself? The sweet, beautiful woman with the blue eyes and legs for days will never be mine, no matter how much I want to possess her.

Well, I sure as hell don't want to spend tonight alone, especially with her out having fun. I need to blow off some steam, drink till this ache in my chest fades. There's only one thing to do: call my best friend, Lucas. I locate his number on my contact list and press the call button, determined to forget Tessa, even as her beautiful face and beaming smile flash in my mind. The vision makes me smile too.

"Barclay," Lucas shouts over loud background noise. "What you doing, man?"

"Calling you."

"But not Barbie." *Great.* He had to mention her. "She's been waiting for your call too."

"Yeah, paying for a date isn't for me," I confess, and regret asking Lucas in the first place. Lesson learned.

"So, everything worked out?"

"Not really." I want to tell him about what happened with Tessa, but he'd probably tell me to run away, like I did, bringing me full circle to the reason I'm talking to him. "Where are you?"

"PH-D at the Dream Hotel. You should come down and join us."

I hear a woman's muffled giggle, and ask, "Us?"

"The usual crowd. Lance and Alex from the firm, along with a few hot blondes. Whatta ya say?"

"I don't know." I stand up and pace to the window. The setting sun reflects an amber color off the mirrored buildings as night starts to fall.

"You've been working too hard, Barc. When was the last time you had fun, or got laid, for that matter?"

When was it? There's been no one since Amanda and I broke up two months ago. No wonder my nerves feel frayed.

I have two choices, and neither one of them appeal to me. Head back to my apartment, drink too much bourbon, and jack off, like I've been doing for too long. The other option is meeting Lucas at the club, and I know what usually happens after a night out with him. I wake up to find a woman in my bed the next morning, but at least it isn't empty.

I cradle the back of my neck and close my eyes. "Okay, I'll meet you there. I need to go home and change."

"Better throw back a few shots before you get here," Lucas adds with a laugh. "We're at least three drinks ahead of you."

Drinks mixed with hot, willing women. This is going to

be a big mistake, but I'm not going to sit around by myself tonight. I have an itch that can only be scratched by the touch of a woman's hand, the feel of her lips, and the softness of her skin. Lucas is right. I need to get laid.

"Don't worry. I'll catch up with you lushes." I grab my jacket off the back of my chair and head out into the night.

18

TESSA

"It's been over thirty minutes, and he still hasn't texted me back," I say to Maggie on the phone. I'm leaning against the headboard in my hotel room with the white comforter surrounding me like a cocoon. "I shouldn't have listened to you. Now I'll never hear from him again."

I pull the phone away from my ear and glance at the screen, double-checking in case a text arrived within the last couple seconds. *Nope.* There's been nothing from Barclay since I mentioned my stupid drink date. Big mistake.

"He asked what you were doing tonight for a reason," Maggie says in her usual, easy-breezy way. "Believe me, he wants you, and probably freaked out that he's not your date."

"Remember, he kicked me to the curb." At least, that's how it felt yesterday when he drove off and left me standing on the sidewalk. It still stings.

"Then you find chocolate-covered strawberries in your room. He comps all your food at the hotel. Gives you the direct emails of executives to help you find a job," she rattles off the ways Barclay's shown he might care for me, but it doesn't make his goodbye any less painful. "I have good money on him showing up before the weekend's over. After all, he owns the hotel, along with the keys to the rooms."

"Like he's going to just bust in here. Believe me, we're over before it even started. I know it's the virgin thing. Different guy. Same scenario."

"He's into you and will come around. Please, just trust me, Tessa. You'll kiss your Prince Charming, but first, you have to meet a frog named Trevor for a drink."

"He's more a toad." I close my eyes and shake my head. I hate having to meet Trevor, especially after Barclay's warning, but I'm going to keep my word so he'll stay silent. "Promise you'll remember to call me at nine o'clock with horrible, date-ending news. I don't care what you have to make up. I can't be in that guy's presence more than thirty minutes, tops."

"I've got your back," she says, and I pray she does.

We end our call. Now, it's time to get ready for this stupid drink date. I decide to wear my dark skinny jeans and a cream-colored top with pink lace overlay. It's sleeveless with spaghetti straps. The bodice cuts across my breasts, showing a non-slutty amount of cleavage, and the hem flows free around my waist. I slip on a pair of nude strappy heeled sandals to complete the look.

I wore subtle makeup for job-hunting today, so I need to up my game for the evening. I apply some muted brown eye shadow for depth, and swipe on a little blush for a healthy pink glow. Next, I comb through my hair with my fingers, then give myself a once over in the bathroom mirror.

There's a lot of bare skin showing and I don't want to give Mr. Spears the wrong idea, so I grab my cream twill jacket to cover my shoulders. It's stylish and fitted at the waist. For the finishing touch, I add a sheer pink lip gloss. Good enough.

As I grab the door handle to exit my room, I hear a text coming in on my phone. It's probably Maggie. I glance at the screen and lean against the door, my heart fluttering. *Barclay.*

Not happy about your date.

Holy crap. Not only did he answer me back, he told me how he felt. I smile because I worried he didn't care, but he must, or he wouldn't be unhappy.

I feel all bouncy inside with nerves and indecision, but my date with Trevor isn't a real date like he probably thinks. It's just what Maggie told me to say. This time, I'll use my own words and no games. I don't know how to play them anyway.

Just drinks and I'm ending it early.

The text bubbling ripples a few seconds, and I wait for his reply.

Why?

He's not you.

No he's not.

I wish he were ...

Me too.

I don't know how to respond, so I wait a couple minutes for him to continue and fill in the blanks behind his comment, but nothing comes. I take a deep breath and exhale the disappointment. It's time to make my way down to the hotel bar.

I arrive in the lobby at the exact time I told Mr. Spears I'd meet him. If he was early, I didn't want to spend a moment more than I had to with him. It's going to feel like an eternity until Maggie calls with some concocted catastrophe requiring me to leave anyway.

I check my phone one last time as I stop at the restaurant entrance off the lobby. Nothing shows up from Barclay. He doesn't like the idea of me with anyone, but doesn't make any attempt to be with me either. Does he realize these back and forth moods of his are tearing up my emotions? Now I know why people call these unrequited feelings a crush.

Another sigh leaves my lips as I peek into the restaurant and see Mr. Spears leaning against the bar. He's dressed in jeans and a long-sleeved gray shirt, and carries himself in a polished style. If I saw him like this from afar for the first time, I'd have rated him a solid nine on the hot, older guy scale. Problem is, I've heard him speak in veiled sexual references while his unwelcomed eyes touched me all over.

I take a deep breath and place one foot in front of the other. It's time to get this night under way.

19

TESSA

A Cheshire cat grin spreads across Mr. Spears' face as he spots me moving toward him. He pushes off the edge of the bar, standing tall, and licks his lips as he scans over my body. *Again.*

"You made it." He reaches out for my hand, but I stick mine inside my front pocket. I don't want to encourage touching tonight. Trying to recover from my rejection, he drops his arm and pulls out the stool next to him. "Have a seat."

"Thanks, Mr. Spears," I say as I sit on the stool.

"Please, call me Trevor. Mr. Spears is what people call my father, and besides, you don't work for me." He slides next to me and wraps his arm around the back of my stool. I move forward on my seat as far as possible, cringing as he scoots his chair closer to mine. The creep is creeping.

"You need a drink," he declares, signaling to the busy bartender.

"Okay, but just one." I'd love a shot or two to get my nerves under control, but can't risk getting too buzzed. I need to keep full command of my senses.

The bartender from two nights ago moves in front of me. "Hey, I remember you," he says with a friendly smile, then turns to Trevor and narrows his eyes. It appears the friendly bartender isn't a big fan of my drink date either. "Are you here with Spears?"

"Just for a drink," I add quickly, and swear the bartender appears relieved.

"Prosecco?" the bartender asks.

"Yes, please," I reply. The bartender turns and grabs a champagne glass, then heads to a cooler.

"He knows you, and so does Barclay," Trevor says, rubbing his chin. "Interesting. I still don't understand why you left with Barclay in his town car, not to mention while barely dressed."

"I was just helping him for the afternoon," I say.

"I bet you helped him," Trevor jeers his voice full of sarcasm. "Anyway, you're here now and Barclay isn't. I'd say I'm the winner tonight."

"Your drink." The bartender places a glass of bubbling liquid in front of me. "On your tab, Spears?"

Trevor nods and returns his eyes back to me. "Let's have a toast." He picks up his highball glass, and I do the same with my champagne flute.

"To chance meetings," he says.

His words twist in my heart. Barclay sat at this very bar two nights ago. It was the first of our chance meetings. Trevor clinks my glass. I want to drink my prosecco in one full swipe, but I just take a sip.

"So, you're looking for a job in the city," he says, though it's an obvious answer since he helped route my résumé.

"Yeah. Just graduated college."

"Where?" Trevor asks.

"University of Montevalo. It's a small college, around twenty-five hundred." I play with the cocktail napkin in front of me, trying to avoid eye contact with him.

"Oh, it's in Spain, right? That's rather impressive." He's wrong, of course, since it's in the small town of Montevalo, Alabama. There is Spanish moss there, but still, he's way off.

"Not quite," I reply.

"Wait. It's in Portugal," he concludes, totally convinced he knows everything. I roll my eyes and shrug. There's no need to contradict him.

Trevor drones on about his job as Hammond Press' chief financial officer. His position sounds important and fits his gigantic ego, though I had no idea he was so high up on the executive scale. Here I was worried about how Barclay's help would raise questions about me. It's likely worse with Trevor, because inexperienced girls from Alabama only get references from chief officers via a family member or blow jobs, and the latter is more this guy's style.

I sigh knowing there's nothing I can do. I catch myself twirling my hair and looking over my shoulder. There's a big, delusional part of me that hopes Barclay will show up and rescue me.

About five inches from my fingers, my phone sits on the bar counter and lights up with an incoming text. *It's Barclay.* I'm anxious to read it, but when I try to reach for my phone, without being too obvious, Trevor says something that diverts my attention.

"Oh, I spoke with Helen Ratner," he says, pausing. My eyes flash to his face, and I hold my breath. His smirk feels like a drum roll as I wait for him to continue. "You should be hearing from her soon. That's all I know. Helen doesn't discuss the marketing side of the company with me."

"Thank you," I say. "You didn't have to do that."

"Well, I couldn't let a beautiful woman down," he says with a tease. I flinch when he reaches out for a strand of my hair. "Besides, I can think of a few things you could do to show me your gratitude."

He's repulsive. There's absolutely no way I can wait until Maggie's call to get rid of him. This guy needs to be put in his place now. He doesn't realize I have tons of experience dealing with creeps like him.

"Oh, what do you have in mind?" I look through my lashes, inching closer to him. His breath still reminds me of garlic.

"Maybe we could take our discussion upstairs?" He waggles his brows, and my stomach turns. *Ugh.*

"You want to sleep with me?" I soften my voice and lower my head. I can't look at him anymore. He probably thinks I'm shy or embarrassed, but I'm trying to hide the obvious disgust on my face.

"I'd be the best you've ever had," he brags, and I bite my lip to keep from laughing out loud.

It's time to make an unmistakable point with my killer high heels. I take a deep breath, mentally prepping myself. The last time I pulled this stunt on a guy, he cried out for his mother. I may seem like a helpless young woman, but Trevor doesn't know my police officer brother, Miles, taught me how to defend myself.

I rise off my stool, push it under the bar, and stand next to him. Trevor follows my motions, licking his lips.

I glance down at his black loafers, a thinner leather than his dress shoes from yesterday. This fact makes me smile. I take half a step closer to him, our bodies almost touching. His eyes darken and breath quickens.

I step in front of him, facing the bar, lift my right foot, and place my spiky heel on the top of his shoe. I press down into the leather, connecting with his flesh, and twist, giving him a fuck-off-you-bastard smile the entire time.

"What the hell are you doing?" he shouts. The other guests around us turn their heads our way.

"Let me set things straight," I hiss in warning. "First, I

don't owe you anything. Second, you're a jerk." I twist and press again. His eyes beg me to release him from the pain.

I dig my heel into his foot one last time and throw what's left of my prosecco at his distressed face. Drops of the sweet liquid run down his cheeks like tears.

As Trevor wipes the drink from his face, he focuses on something behind me. His eyes go wide in surprise—or is it fear? Before I can turn around and see what has his attention, Barclay is standing next to me.

"What the hell is going on here?" Barclay asks through gritted teeth. He wraps his large hand around Trevor's forearm and tugs him away from me.

Barclay's jaw and neck muscles look like they may snap. His ebony eyes blaze as he glances between Trevor and me, and his tousled black hair matches his shirt and jeans. He resembles an angry knight in dark armor, making my knees weak like some swoony maiden.

"Trevor and I got off on the wrong foot," I answer with a victorious grin.

20

"What did he do to you?" I ask Tessa, my grip on Trevor's arm tightening as I imagine the possibilities.

"I didn't touch her. *Cousin,*" Trevor spits the last word out like a venomous snake. He tries to jerk his arm away, but there's no way in hell I'm letting go of him yet.

"Cousin?" Tessa whispers, eyes wide in disbelief. I nod my head, though I wish I could deny it. Her beautiful pink lips form a perfect circle.

"Where's Caroline?" It's my turn to spit at Trevor, my voice laced with accusation.

"We're taking a break." He avoids my eyes as he speaks,

lying his ass off. His girlfriend deserves better, and I hope she figures that out soon.

"Get the hell out of here." I release Trevor's arm in disgust. If we weren't in a public place that carries my last name, I'd clock him for whatever he did to make Tessa douse him with her drink. She's feisty, but not violent. He must've crossed the line. It's his M.O. with women.

"You might out rank me at Hammond, but you can't order me around here," he jeers, his chin held high.

"Let's call Caroline and see what she thinks." I dig my phone out of my back pocket, press my passcode into the screen, and wave it in front of Trevor. I narrow my eyes at him and wait, seeing if he'll call my bluff.

"Okay, fine," he says, lowering his shoulders in defeat. He grabs a few cocktail napkins off the bar and wipes off his face, then his shirt.

Trevor begins to walk away, but stops in his tracks after a few paces. He spins around to face Tessa and me. I wrap my arm around her small waist and pull her into my side.

"Until next time, Tessa," Trevor says in a seductive tone. When our eyes meet, a mocking smile slides across his face.

"There won't be a *fucking* next time. You understand me?" I hiss at him.

"I understand *way* more than you," he laughs while looking at Tessa. Feeling her stiffen in my arms, I glance down at her and find her gaze focused on the floor. *What the hell is up?*

Trevor shakes his head. "See you later, cousin," he mocks, and turns to leave the bar. Good riddance.

"Are you all right?" I ask Tessa, inspecting her from head to toe. She's stunning in her high heels and tight jeans, and doesn't show any obvious signs of harm.

"Yeah, I'm good." She gazes up at me through her lashes like I saved her from a predator. But I feel like I'm the dangerous one right now as adrenaline races through my veins.

Her innocent beauty and the feel of her curves under my fingertips do crazy things to me. I want throw her over my shoulder, take her upstairs, and fuck her senseless.

Christ, help me.

I call the bartender over to order a drink, but he beats me to the punch and sets a tall shot of bourbon down in front of me.

"Thought you'd need this," he says.

I release my right arm from around Tessa and throw back the amber liquid. The bartender refills my shot glass, and I drink its contents down even faster.

"Are you okay, Barclay?" Tessa says, standing next to me, eyes filled with worry. She places a hand on my forearm in an effort to comfort me. She has no idea how dangerous I could be to her.

When I passed by the restaurant and recognized Tessa standing at the bar alongside my asshole cousin, my vision turned red and I nearly ran to her side.

Yes, sweetheart, I'm anything but okay. I've lost a battle of control. With myself.

I sit down on a barstool and reach for her hands. She gasps as I pull her between my legs, our faces close together. She stares at me with big blue eyes full of hope and desire. I pray I've made the right decision.

"I tried to stay away from you." I trace her cheek and the line of her jaw with the slightest touch. "But as you can see, it's become impossible."

"I'm glad," she whispers, leaning in to my touch, a slight shiver running over her skin.

"We'll see," I say in warning. Her full lips curve in a teasing smile, inducing visions of her kneeling before me. My cock presses against the zipper of my jeans, and it hurts so damn good.

All these dirty thoughts of her running through my head make one thing pretty damn clear: I could totally ruin her before she heads back to Alabama in a few days. Hell, even if she does find a job here, I'm not the man for her. I'm too old and she's too chaste. Not to mention, she's definitely not the kind of woman to fuck and toss away. She's a keeper. I just wish I had the privilege of making her mine.

21

TESSA

I stand between Barclay's bent legs as he sits on the edge of his barstool. His dark eyes are velvety night, sensuous and full of promises I can't even fathom, but I feel them. He has the key to an unknown part of me, and I need him to unlock it before I combust into a million pieces.

I want to touch him, place my hands on his muscular thighs, feel their strength under my fingertips, but should I? Is that too forward? I have no idea what a man with his experience expects from a woman. Just as I prepare to move my fingers, my phone sings "Sweet Home Alabama" and vibrates on the wooden bar top. Cringing, I grab my phone and silence the ringer.

It's Maggie. She's calling right on schedule, and I can't wait to tell her what happened and who's with me now. It's like she peered into a crystal ball and knew the future.

I hold up my index finger and point to the phone in my hand. "I need to get this. It's my best friend." Barclay nods, but remains impassive. I don't think he likes the interruption, and neither do I, but she'll keep calling if I don't answer it.

"Maggie," I say, my voice turning into a whisper. "The crisis has been averted."

"What do you mean? The toad has hopped away?" she asks.

"Yes. I applied the spiked heel defense. I couldn't wait for your call. He tried to get me to sleep with him." The thought of Trevor's words and breath make me shudder in disgust.

"I should've punched him," Barclay practically roars while standing up from his barstool. I guess I wasn't quiet enough. Gone is the reflective man who confessed his attraction toward me. It's like he's turned into a hot version of the Incredible Hulk, dressed in all black with perfect hair and a tense jawline. "I told you to stay away from him, that he was bad news."

"I handled him just fine," I say, fumbling with my words. I feel breathless and so turned on by Barclay's show of male possessiveness.

"Like hell," Barclay replies, still grasping my left hand.

"Wait," Maggie yells into the phone, shaking me out of the testosterone haze. "Is that *Barclay* you're talking to?"

"Mmmhmmm," I answer with a hum of happiness, because the beautiful man I never thought I'd see again towers over me, and I want to fold into him so bad and never let go. Only yesterday, I'd cried, heartbroken, thinking being with him was an improbable dream. Now, he holds my hand, and without knowing it, my heart. I feel free, vulnerable, and confused. He's almost too much to handle.

"I told you he'd come back around," Maggie says, full of glee. I can almost hear her jumping up and down. "Okay, get off the phone and quit disagreeing with him. Have sex first, then fight, and then have angry sex. It's amazing."

"Bye, Maggie." I end the call and toss my phone in my bag. My mind's already flooded with dirty thoughts, so I don't need to add hers.

I look up at Barclay, and he slightly raises his eyebrows as he peers down at me. I can't tell whether he's amused or upset.

Wait. Surely he didn't overhear what Maggie said? A flush crosses over my face at the thought.

"Um, thanks for getting rid of Trevor ... I mean, Mr. Spears." A corner of his mouth tips up. He's gloating at my admission that he was right. I did need his help in the end to make Trevor disappear for good.

Barclay hands me my champagne flute. His long fingers encircle the glass, and I can barely see the bubbling liquid inside it. The bartender must've refilled my prosecco after I tossed it on Trevor. Bless his heart.

"Be a good girl and drink this," he says, his smoldering gaze fixed on me. What a beautiful, bossy man.

I bring the glass to my lips and down it in a couple long sips. Barclay's perfect mouth eases into a lazy smile. He enjoys watching me submit to his demands. I don't know why, but I want to obey them. He takes the empty glass from me and sets it down on the bar.

"Michael," Barclay says, and the bartender turns our way. "Put all these drinks on my tab, including Trevor's, and add forty percent for your trouble."

"Thanks for the drink," I say.

"It's nothing." He shrugs. "I own the joint."

"So I heard," I joke, and he shakes his head with a slight chuckle.

"Tell me, Tessa. Do you have any more so called 'drink dates' this evening?" He gives me a wink, and I blush like the silly girl from Alabama I am. No one has ever really winked at me. Well ... no one over six feet tall and handsome enough to land on a billboard. "Are there any more suitors I need to fight off?"

He's teasing me with his words, and then his touch, as his fingers trace small circles on the inside of my wrist. It feels like he's touching me everywhere. I can't imagine what it would feel like if he actually kissed me. I seriously might faint. I'll never laugh at the word "swoon" again, that's for sure. It's become my permanent state around him.

"Let me check my calendar." I smile up at him and

shimmy my shoulders. He narrows his eyes, then gives me a sexy smirk. He realizes it's my turn to tease him.

"Then you're all mine now, and coming with me."

Whoa. Did he just say I'm his?

He weaves his fingers through one of my hands and pulls me away from the bar. We start walking toward the exit to the lobby.

"Wait. Where are you taking me?"

"On the best damn drink date of your life."

22

Tessa

Hand in hand, Barclay hustles me out of the restaurant into the hotel lobby. I trail behind him by a step and try to catch up, but his long strides make it impossible. I give his hand a yank before he starts dragging me along the shiny marble floor.

He peers over his shoulder with a mischievous spark in his eye. "Having trouble keeping up?"

I shoot him a menacing glare, and he stops dead in his tracks. *Finally.*

"I can only go so fast in these heels. Not to mention, you're a giant compared to me."

"I should just throw you over my shoulders. It seems like

something a giant would do after scaring away your date and making you mine."

"You wouldn't."

"Which side would you like, the right or left?"

"Barclay," I breathe … or more like moan. The idea of him going caveman sounds hot as hell and makes me dizzy.

"I'm in a mood tonight, little girl." His dark eyes are set on smolder, and he moves toward me, like a tiger ready to pounce.

Before I can even blink, Barclay wraps his hands around my waist and hoists me up to his shoulder. Thanks to gravity and a gentle push of his hand on my lower back, I bend and grab for something, anything, to anchor myself. My hands find his firm, denim-covered ass. I squeeze him and let out a squeal. It's the first time I've touched a man in a forbidden zone. I hook my thumbs inside his back pockets and hang on.

Barclay begins to walk forward, and I bounce in rhythm to his cadence. I raise my head, and my hair swishes around my face like a moving curtain. People gasp and mutter all around us, because why wouldn't they? I want to peek out and see their expressions, since I'm sure hot guys carrying their dates around like this happens all the time in Manhattan. I snort at my own thoughts, then splay my hands over his hard cheeks and try to push up so I can see the people in the lobby.

Everyone, including the doormen and bellhops, are

standing still with their eyes flashing between my face and Barclay.

"Oh my God, Barclay. Someone's taking photos of us." I turn my face away to avoid the man with his phone aimed at us. Thankfully, Barclay picks up his pace as we come to the hotel exit.

The same doorman who wouldn't give me a smile the other morning, sends me a thumbs-up. I wave at him as we pass by. Talk about awkward.

"Stay down," Barclay commands as he walks us through the spinning turnstile door.

Once outside, and a few steps later, he swats me on my bottom, and I squeal again. It's the first time a man's touched me *there*.

After placing his hands on my hips, he eases me down the front of his body until my feet meet the sidewalk. I gaze up into his eyes as he wraps his arms around me.

"What just happened?" I ask, because his behavior confuses me. Yesterday, he left me here on the sidewalk without looking back, and now he's hauling me out of a hotel like a sack of potatoes.

"I let go," he says, with an exhilarating smile. One I've never seen on him before.

"How did this letting go thing feel?"

"Damn good." He bends down and kisses my forehead. I feel the light caress of his lips all the way to my toes. He releases me from his hold and grabs my hand. "But we'll probably make Page Six."

"What's that?" An uneasy feeling twists in my stomach. The word "but" doesn't sound good.

"The New York Post's gossip page. Something I try to avoid," he says in a dismissive tone, but I freeze in place, afraid of the fallout for me.

"What if my brother sees it? He'll be on the next plane here to fetch me home."

"Don't worry. No one knows who you are unless I tell them, and I won't." I say a little prayer that I turned my head in time to avoid a direct shot of my face.

There isn't a driver or car at the curb waiting for us. Instead, Barclay hails a cab and we climb inside. He tells the cab driver the address and sits back in his seat.

"You're too far away." He wraps his arm around me and pulls me across the seat to his side.

A small voice, probably my mother's, warns me to put on my seatbelt, but I ignore it. I've never felt safer in my life than in his arms. Besides, he smells divine.

I close my eyes, then breathe in and out, and the most contented feeling washes over me. "Where are we going?"

"We're headed to PH-D to meet my friend, Lucas."

"Maggie, my best friend who plans on coming to New York City, keeps talking about this club. She put it on our top ten list of bars to hit once we land here permanently. She knows more about nightlife than me." I pause and glance up at Barclay.

Our faces are inches apart, and our lips are even closer. What I wouldn't give to have him kiss me. He stares at my mouth, his eyes ravenous, and licks his lips, then looks away. I deflate, but try to recover ... by talking. *Thank you, hot male induced anxiety.*

"Anyway, she told me the rope lines to get in places like this are nuts and bouncers get to pick and choose who enters."

"No rope lines or bouncers for us. We'll be taking the service elevator upstairs. Standard VIP stuff. I hope this isn't a disappointment." A corner of his mouth tips up. He's cockier than I thought.

"Are you kidding? Maggie's going to turn green when I tell her this."

"How long are you planning on staying here, in the city?" Barclay asks, and if that isn't the two-thousand-dollar question—which is likely how much money I'll need to stay longer. I don't think seven days is going to be enough time to get a job, especially since I'm working from ground zero.

"Thanks to you and the emails you gave me, I have a couple interviews next week, but my flight back to Alabama leaves on Wednesday afternoon."

"That's great." He rubs his chin and sighs. "But you'll need more time. Listen. Stay an extra week on me. Well ... not on me, exactly," Barclay mutters the last part, appearing flustered.

"You're way too kind, and have already done more than enough to help me," I say, declining. I can't take him up on this offer. Well ... not for the hotel at least, though the other "on me" part has definite possibilities. "I'll figure it out."

"Just know the offer stands if you need it."

"Thank you," I say, and wonder if I should ignore my silly pride and say yes. But my first interview is Monday, so waiting to see how things go is the better option, and my pride stays intact—for now.

"Tell me about this brother of yours."

"Miles." I sigh. I don't even know where to begin. Overprotective doesn't even scratch the surface with him. "He's my big brother, and also about your height and build, but with blond hair and a police badge."

"He's a police officer?" Barclay stiffens, and it's not in a good way. *Ugh.* Here we go.

"Yes. My father's the sheriff of Monroeville too." I lay all the badges on the table.

"Okay," he says, running his hand through his dark locks. "This explains a lot."

"As in my lack of experience with men," I add before I can stop myself. But we might as well lay the fact that I've never been laid on the table too—especially if he wants what I want: me in his bed.

The cab comes to a stop before he can respond, saving me from further self-induced humiliation. I glance out the window as he pays. The sidewalk's jammed with scores of young people. It looks like a stiletto factory.

Barclay defies the laws of nature as I watch his large frame ease out of the cab. It's more like he floats on the surface. Me? It takes a couple pushes to scoot to the door. He holds out his hand when I peek my head out.

"Let's go," he says, but it sounds like a grumble of regret.

I place my hand in his, but the look in his eyes makes worry rise up inside me. It reminds me of yesterday on the sidewalk, like he's back to the tug of war between walking away from me or being the one who cashes in my V-card.

23

PH-D bursts with kinetic energy. Music vibrates with a rhythmic beat. People fill every inch of the space, raving with their hands in the air. Strobe lights flash off faces and walls while hedonistic desires fill the smoky air.

The atmosphere is wild and mesmerizing, exactly as I remembered from years ago. After I woke up from the party haze that filled my twenties, I swore I'd never walk through these doors again. Yet here I am, blending into the scenery like a weekly regular.

I'm parked on a leather couch next to Lucas. A glass of bourbon in my hand, and our special VIP section hidden in darkness, detached from the thumping crowds. The staff waits on our every beck and call, as they should for the price we're paying for bottle service. But all the glitzy trimmings and gyrating bodies don't distract me from my main attraction: Tessa. She's dancing without a care in front of me alongside Lucas's hookup for the night.

Tessa discards her jacket and tosses it in my direction on the couch. Her blond hair spills over her exposed shoulders and down her back. Her full breasts bounce and hips sway with the music. The pulse of the club pounds against my skin, but all my senses laser on her. I shift my weight in the seat, but nothing helps ease my craving for her.

When Tessa beams at me, I can't breathe, because I realize where the source of her smile comes from. *Pure joy.* It's from her heart, not something based on all the lust and booze being sold at the club. She radiates what's missing here. Genuine happiness.

As the place continues to hum, I continue to watch Tessa move her delectable body. Her innocently seductive actions make my breath quicken and my heart race. I can no longer deny one fact: her hypnotic beauty has me under its spell.

I have no business falling for her, and not just because of her inexperience, which freaks me out. The main problem is she's only temporary. Nothing is permanent. It's like meeting that hot girl on a spring break hookup and promising you'll call her when you get back to your college, knowing full well you'll never see her again.

As much as I want to do wicked things to Tessa while she's in the city looking for a job, I can't forget she's someone's daughter and sister. The way she speaks about her family tells me they love her dearly. Who wouldn't? I've changed since I last stepped foot into this club. I'm older now, and said goodbye to my player ways years ago, unlike Lucas, who'll fuck any woman without a thought beyond getting off.

I rake my hands through my hair, wondering why a thirty-seven-year-old man is worrying about a young woman's family. Hell, I haven't even kissed her yet, but damn if I can't imagine what it will be like when I finally do. Tonight, her head won't hit the pillow without me tasting her sweet lips.

"She's just ..." Lucas interrupts my thoughts with a drunken slur.

A quick glance at Lucas finishes his sentence. He's gaping at Tessa with his tongue practically sticking out of his mouth. She's having the same effect on him. Neither of us can look away. Still, he needs to check himself, so I nudge him in the rib with my elbow.

"Ouch," he shouts, rubbing his side.

"Watch your eyes," I yell over the music.

"It's kind of hard. She's a fucking goddess. Guys would pay just to watch her move like this. Even fully clothed."

Tessa's downing her third glass of prosecco, making it her fourth for the night, and her inhibitions have loosened with each and every sip. Me? I've never sipped bourbon this slow, a calculated choice, since we're both going back to the Hammond for the night.

"I've never seen this one at the escort service." Lucas gives me a wicked smile. "Believe me, I'd have been first if I had."

"Got to hell, Lucas. She's not a piece of meat for you to paw at." A rush of anger races through my veins, and I curl my free hand into a fist. "She's from the South, not an escort service."

"Well, what do you know? You like her. A lot," Lucas marvels, holding up his hands. "But seriously, where did you find her? One-eight-hundred-jail-bait?"

"Don't be stupid. She's over twenty-one."

"Barely." Lucas gives me a pointed look. "Does she work at Hammond Press?"

"Are you kidding me? You know the rules," I huff. It's the reason I've given her leads for other companies. "Besides, I don't mix my work and personal life. It never ends wells."

"Tell me about it, but I'd make an exception to get in those jeans." I flash him an evil eye and the side of his lips tip up. "Okay, Romeo. How did you meet her?"

"Over coffee." Well ... spilt coffee, but the details aren't important.

I lock eyes with Tessa, and she beams back at me. Her hair and skin glow under the lights. She crooks a finger at me, wanting me to join her. I bite my lip and nod at her. What I'd like to do is take her back to the hotel and kiss her within an inch of her life, along with every inch of her skin.

"Huh? Like this angel just fell down from heaven into your lap."

"Pretty much." I pull a wad of cash out of my wallet and

give it to Lucas for the bill. "We're outta here." I rise off the couch to join the blonde bombshell, drawing me to her like a moth to a flame.

"I had a courier leave the Yankee tickets at the hotel front desk. See you Sunday." I release a deep breath. Dammit. I forgot I said I'd go to the game with him.

"Sure, Lucas." I sigh, knowing I can't back out this late, but I only have a few days left with Tessa. I need her to take me up on the offer to stay longer at the hotel, at least until she finds a job. I want her here permanently. "It's after midnight. I'd better get Cinderella home."

"Lucky fuck," he scoffs.

"Yeah. I am," I say, walking toward Tessa with a cocky grin.

24

TESSA

Barclay sets his empty glass on a side table and finally rises off the couch to join me on the floor. I've been dancing with his friend's date, and Barclay seemed way too comfortable watching me, but I loved having his eyes on me. Between his hungry stares and the intense energy filling the air, I've never felt more alive and wild, but I'd rather have Barclay's arms around me and his lips on mine. A girl can at least hope that's the direction the night's heading.

Barclay leans forward and brings his mouth to my ear. When his lips caress my heated skin with a feather-like touch, tingles ghost down my neck and a warmth pools deep in my belly. I can only take so much anticipation before I end up begging him to kiss me and humiliating myself in the process.

"Okay, princess. It's time to go," he says, pulling away from me, but I want him back close enough so I can smell his delicious scent. The look in his eyes tells me the night's not over yet, which thrills me, but there's one thing I want to do first. With a dreamy man. In my dream city.

"Dance with me," I breathe, batting my eyelashes at him and adding a lip bite.

I may be lacking in hands-on experience, but I've read enough romance novels to have a clue about the art of seduction and sexual persuasion. His dark hooded eyes signal I've hit the mark, and I breathe a sigh of relief.

"Just one," he says, taking my hands and pulling me to him, a teasing gleam in his eyes. I won this round.

Reaching up, I join my hands around the nape of his neck, basking in the feel of his skin after I've been dying to touch him all night. My forefingers twirl his hair at the base of his collar. It's soft, yet thick, with a slight flip on the ends. Maggie would call it sex hair, and I would have to agree.

A new song begins, and I tighten my hands around him. "One more song, please? That one was just ending."

"Okay, but after that, we leave." I smile up at him in victory.

Barclay rests a hand on the small of my back, his other possessively holding my neck. He presses me closer to him, and our bodies mold together. I feel the hard lines of his erection against my stomach, and gasp, though he doesn't press hard against me. It's more of an introduction, an extremely firm hello. He responds with a twisted grin, then his dark gaze lands on my lips.

Kiss me, Barclay. Please just kiss me.

But he doesn't. Instead, his hips start a sensuous swivel in time with the beat, and I follow his lead.

A week ago, back in Monroeville, Alabama, a dance like this with a handsome older man would've scared me senseless or gotten him run out of town by my brother. But here, at this club in New York City, our erotic movements match our surroundings—daring and living on the edge.

"The things I want to do to you, sweet girl," he whispers against my ear. I close my eyes, and my head falls back. "I'll start with a kiss. One you'll still feel on your lips tomorrow morning."

"Yes." I slur the word in a haze of desperation and lick my lips at the thought of finally kissing this beautiful man. I rise up on my tiptoes so he can reach me better.

"Not here, for all the world to see. I want to take my time in private." I sigh out of sheer frustration. *How much can a girl take?*

"Screw the song." I release my hands from around his neck and wrap my fingers around one of his hands. "We're leaving. Now."

Barclay chuckles as I drag him through the crowd of partiers. I'm a woman on a mission and make a beeline straight toward the service elevator.

Barclay and I are alone in the elevator as we descend to

the main floor. He moves closer, essentially backing me into a corner, and looms over me. I hold my breath as I look into his heavy-lidded eyes. They give me a thrill of excitement mixed with a touch of fear, but more of myself, because I could totally let loose with him.

Then what?

There are no guarantees. Barclay could be nothing more than a memory I carry with me for the rest of my life. My first. But it's time I quit overanalyzing. It's keeping me from living my life, and I want to live in the moment for once. Feel it. Breathe it. Be with him and forget about tomorrow. Somewhere in Alabama, I imagine Maggie giving me a fist pump.

"I can't stop thinking about one thing." He breaks the silence and rests both hands above me on each side of the corner walls. I blink and wait, wanting him to tell me more. "How has no man touched you yet? You're the most beautiful creature sent by some wicked twist of fate to torture me. I should let you go—let you find someone your own age."

Ouch, that stings. *And how do I even respond to something like this?* It seems obvious to me that there's been an undeniable pull, like a force of nature, joining us together from the moment we looked into each other's eyes.

Maybe with his years of experience with women, what I feel is nothing new to him. But to me, it means everything. I'll play his "I'm too old for you" game and see if I can erase his hesitations of us being together once and for all. It's not like I'm asking for more than tonight anyway.

A true fact about southern women: we know how to fight for what we want. It comes from living with frizz-inducing humidity and being raised on Lynyrd Skynyrd. Both build fierce determination.

"All right, Barclay. I'll only date guys in their twenties. Any suggestions? I'm sure you have a few who would fit the bill." I square my shoulders, and anger flashes in Barclay's eyes. His jaw tightens and his lips form a straight line.

"We'll finish this conversation in the cab," he growls.

My dating declaration is like hitting a row of sevens on a slot machine. He's now imagining me with other men, and I want to yell *jackpot!* When the elevator arrives at the ground floor, Barclay leads me outside to the edge of the sidewalk. He hails a cab and ushers me inside. I laugh to myself as he sits down next to me in a huff. This car ride should be loads of fun. *For real.*

25

TESSA

Barclay grumbles the hotel address to the cabbie and I lean against the door, twirling my hair around a finger, waiting for him to speak to me. After we barrel through a couple city blocks, he turns toward me. Our eyes meet, and he exhales a deep breath. His jaw is more relaxed, and his eyes are no longer throwing flames my way, but he still looks intense and on edge.

"Tessa, I don't want to talk about you with other men. At. All. But since you brought it up, let me school you on some facts."

"Please do," I scoff, trying to act brave.

"Things move fast here. In Manhattan, a guy in his twenties considers dating a woman for a week a long-term relationship. They're getting the feel of having money jingling in their pockets along with other things. They're as shallow as a baby pool with only one thing on their mind." Barclay raises a brow suggestively, obviously meaning sex.

"Not all guys are like that," I say, making a lame attempt at defending the young men in this city, but I wonder if he's right. PH-D was like a sexual playground. Hands wandered, searching the available equipment, and everyone seemed okay with it.

"Trust me," he says with a sigh, running his hand through his thick hair. Oh, how I itch to touch those soft strands again.

"Okay," I concede. "Twenties are out, so I'll settle for guys in their thirties?" I shrug and wait for his answer, knowing he's thirty-seven.

"Not a good idea either. Too much baggage from their twenties."

Time to play along with his madness. "Well, that leaves teenagers or men in their forties. Which should it be?"

"Have you ever considered becoming a nun?" He smirks at me like it's a joke, but his smile wavers.

"Ugh. You're getting a knuckle sandwich for saying that." I give his bicep a light punch, and he flinches. I roll my eyes at his overreaction to the slight tap, and he throws me a crooked smile. *Whatever.* He's extremely annoying at the moment.

"You sound just like my brother. And the answer is no. I

don't want to be a nun, because I've lived like one throughout high school and college. It's a habit I intend on breaking with someone special and ..." I pause, battling over whether to show my cards or fold them.

His eyes search mine, and I remind myself not to over-think things. Live in the moment. Take risks ... even if it leaves me vulnerable to heartbreak. There's some comfort knowing this time he's in the car with me, instead of leaving me on the sidewalk alone and driving off without a back-ward glance. I take a mental step and jump off a cliff, hoping he'll catch me.

"Barclay, I don't want anyone else but you."

My breathing becomes erratic, and I close my eyes, waiting for his reply. I can't face his possible rejection head-on. My stomach knots as each second passes.

"Open your eyes and look at me, sweet girl," he coaxes me in a voice as smooth as silk. When I do as he bids, a slow smile builds on Barclay's face. "Let's start with that kiss."

"Let's," I breathe.

Barclay pulls me across the backseat and wraps his arm around my shoulders. I melt into him with a contented sigh. This place next to him, being held in his grasp and inhaling his heady scent, feels right, like we were meant to fit together in some grand cosmic design.

"So beautiful." Barclay cups my jaw and tilts my chin up toward his face. His thumb caresses my cheek. The light touch is almost too much to endure. "Are you sure?"

I nod my head, too choked up to speak. All the pent up

desire has left me unable to utter a simple word. His eyes turn smoky black, smoldering, matching the passion I feel inside.

Lowering his head, he brings his lips to mine. It's gentle, a small touch, a whisper of lips on lips. Then, he unleashes something hungry, fast, all-consuming, drawing me tighter into his arms. Any tension within me dissolves on an exhaled sigh of surrender.

When our tongues touch and intertwine, my head spins and an unfamiliar, but welcome, warmth builds low in my belly. The desire for more of him and his sinful lips threatens to consume me.

I run my hand over his chest, feeling the solid wall of muscles under my fingertips. Wanting to explore more of him, I trail higher, tracing the skin above his collar, then farther to his jaw. I travel over the chiseled edges and masculine stubble. He moans into my mouth, and I'm in awe my simple touch moved a man like him.

"Tessa. Tessa," he whispers between passion-filled kisses, and I hum in utter bliss against his lips, not having enough breath to speak.

My body burns for him, and it hits me. Here, somewhere in midtown Manhattan, I experienced my first real kiss from a *real* man. Those guys in college were amateurs. Barclay is perfection.

The cab slows down to a stop, and my eyes flutter open, taking in the front of the hotel. "Can we go around the block one more time?" I plead.

"I have an even better idea." He tosses the cab driver a few bills and takes my hand. "How about I tuck you into bed?"

I gulp, but it's what I want. I think. *Wait*—I'm done thinking. Barclay's the one.

"Okay. My bed I guess? Since we're at the hotel and all." I fumble over my words. *Nervous much, Tessa?* A corner of his lip tips up.

"You know, you're adorable." He opens the door of the cab and helps me out onto the curb.

"Kitten's are adorable," I say with a pout. I get the feeling he's never spoken like this to another woman in Manhattan.

"I'm talking about your sweet innocence." He taps me on the nose, and I roll my eyes. "The rest of you is stunning." He steps back, and his eyes travel over me. "I wouldn't change either. Both combined make you irresistible."

"Thanks." I blush and glance away, trying not to crumble under his wanton perusal.

The cab is long gone, and we're alone on the sidewalk ... well, not totally. People pass by, but no one seems to care about our conversation. He pulls me into his arms, and I look up at him.

"I forgot to tell you something." He pauses a second, gaining my full attention. "I live here."

"Wait. At the Hammond?" He nods, and his disarming smirk is back. "No, you didn't. Believe me, I would've remembered that major detail."

"After the company bought the building, I helped with the redesign. The top ten floors are all residential."

"Let me guess. You're on the top."

"I prefer the top, sweetheart. The views are great." He gives me that damn crooked smile, and I melt. "Let me show you."

We walk into the hotel lobby, and a doorman comes running to Barclay's side. His eyes are wide, darting between Barclay and me.

"Excuse me, sir," the bellman says.

"What's the problem, Peters?" I notice the golden nametag on the bellman's chest.

"It's her, sir," he rushes, pointing his eyes at me. I look up at Barclay, confused, then back to Peters. "Are you Contessa Holly, miss?"

"I am." I tighten my fingers around Barclay's hand. "Did something happen?"

"Well, miss. The hotel manager's upstairs in your room with a couple NYPD."

26

BARCLAY

"Did someone break into her room?" I ask Peters. He's usually the measured, never-cracks-a-smile bellman, but a pair of police officers showing up at the hotel has him rattled. I've never seen him this jumpy.

"Nothing like that, Mr. Hammond. Apparently Miss Holly's brother has been trying to get a hold of her all night and decided to have the police investigate. The NYPD is doing this as a courtesy for her brother since it hasn't been long enough to report a missing person," he rushed out.

"Oh my God," Tessa exclaims in utter shock. "I'm so sorry, Barclay." She releases her hand from mine and cups her face in embarrassment.

"Contessa." I say her full name for the first time. It sounds like royalty and fits her perfectly. "We'll get to the bottom of this. Don't worry. And thank you, Peters. I'll escort Miss Holly up to her room."

"I need to check my phone." Tessa rustles around in her bag with shaky hands as we walk through the lobby to the elevators.

As we stand, waiting, she scrolls through the messages on her phone and shakes her head. She mutters under her breath as she reads each one, and I have no idea what awaits us upstairs. I feel like a teenage boy bringing his date home after her curfew. Hell, it's only twelve thirty, a few strokes past midnight, and early for the city on a Friday night. Apparently she *is* Cinderella, at least to her family. And that makes me the bad wolf in this "southern girl comes to the Big Apple" fairy tale.

"Seventeen missed messages from my mother, brother, and even my father. They escalate from 'how's your evening,' to 'give us a call or we're phoning the police.'" Tessa gazes up at me with cloudy eyes. "I don't want to play my voice messages."

"Understandable." We enter the elevator and I push the button for her floor.

"Oh God." A tear escapes her gorgeous baby blue eyes and falls down her cheek. And with it, a piece of my heart falls harder for this young woman. I don't want her feeling pain ever. I want to shield and protect her, but it's her family.

"Listen, Tessa. It will be okay." I hug her and kiss the top of her hair. Soft silk meets my lips and her sweet scent fills my senses. I close my eyes, drinking all of her in.

This protectiveness of her makes me feel uneasy about the confrontation too. I place my fingers under her chin and tilt her head upward so I can see her face. "I think it's best that I don't appear as your date for the evening. Does that make sense?"

"Yes," she says in a shaky voice. I release my arms around her and wipe the tears from her face. "It will raise too many question. Thank you. I'm the worst date ever."

"Well, having cops at my date's door is a new one for me. But I'm learning there's seldom a dull moment around you," I say with a chuckle. The elevator stops, and the doors open. "Just follow my lead. I've got you, baby."

We exit the elevator and walk down a hallway toward her room. Tessa stays a step behind me. I glance over my shoulder and give her a reassuring smile. We turn a corner, and two uniformed New York City policemen come into view, with the night manager, Josh Presley, on their left.

"Gentlemen," I say, stopping in front of Tessa's room. She's at my side, but partially hiding behind me. "This is Contessa Holly. I've escorted her upstairs after my bellman alerted me to the situation."

"Mr. Hammond. I have Miss Holly's brother on the phone." Presley holds his cell phone up. "He'd like to speak with you."

The policemen stare us down, crossing their arms over their chests, revealing the guns holstered at their waists.

"Let me talk to him and clear everything up," Tessa says, moving toward Presley with her hand outstretched. "I apologize for the inconvenience to ya'll."

"Hold on." Presley brings his cell phone up to his ear. "I suppose you heard all of this, Officer Holly?"

Presley nods his head, looking from Tessa to me. "All right," he says into the phone. "Officer Holly would rather speak to you, Mr. Hammond."

Well, shit. Presley doesn't wait for my reply before handing me the phone. I clear my throat, feeling like a kid being brought before the principal.

"This is Barclay Hammond," I say as my hands begin to sweat.

I glance down at Tessa, and her anxious expression makes me hide mine. She needs my confidence, and frankly, so do I. I give her a slight smile and watch her exhale a deep breath. *Yeah, I've got you, babe.*

"Mr. Hammond. Miles Holly here. I understand you're the owner of the hotel my sister is staying at. Is this correct?" His tone is commanding, and I stifle a scoff at the first question in many to come.

"Yes. I'm the owner," I say. No need to elaborate on specific details until I know how he plans to take this conversation.

"Do you have a curfew for young women?" I try not to laugh at his ludicrous question, but she did mention I was just like him when I asked if she wanted to become a nun. Maybe she should've stayed in a convent while here.

"No. We aren't restrictive in the hours of our guests coming and going."

"Do you have a sister, Mr. Hammond?" he asks.

Miles is damn good at his job, because his question goes right to a soft spot. I try to imagine my sister, Victoria, going to a city like Manhattan all alone at Tessa's age—a gorgeous young woman who hasn't seen the evil of the real world. As a police officer, Miles knows what criminals are capable of, even in a small town like Monroeville. Plus, he likely DVRs every episode of *Law & Order*.

The line is silent as he awaits my answer. Sweet Tessa worries her lip and twists a strand of hair around her finger. I take a couple deep breaths.

"Yes, I do."

"Well, brother to brother, I need you to do me a favor. Can you do this for me, Mr. Hammond?" He pauses, and I have only one answer.

"Of course."

"Her family would be indebted to you. Make sure she's safe while she's there. I was seconds away from booking a plane to New York before she showed up."

Well, dammit. I sigh. He'd have me arrested for indecency by these two officers if he knew I was kissing Tessa only moments ago, and as hard as marble with one plan on my mind.

"Your sister seems like a bright young woman. More than capable of taking care of herself, but I will watch over her as best as I can." I side glance toward Tessa, speaking the truth, as much for my own need as a promise to her brother.

"Thanks again. And tell her to keep her phone turned on."

"Why don't you tell her?" I hand the phone to Tessa and she mouths, *"Thank you."*

She retreats into the open door of her room, and Presley walks behind her, following his phone. The two policemen eye me with suspicion, and I feel like they're reading my mind.

"Well … I guess we're done with everything here." I give them a two-finger salute and head toward the elevator, feeling their eyes on my back as I walk away. I bet they have sisters too. Just my luck.

Once inside my penthouse, I head straight for my bar and pour myself a drink, making it a double. I walk out onto my terrace and recline on a cushioned lounger, staring up at the few stars able to shine through the hazy city lights. The bourbon disappears after a couple swigs. I wanted to share this view with Tessa tonight. Watch her eyes light up as she took in the city's skyline.

I set my glass on the table next to me and run my hands through my hair. How does a thirty-seven-year-old man, after one kiss, get cockblocked by two police officers? Wait— make that three. He chases after a southern belle and somehow becomes her chaperone.

If only Miles knew what I wanted to do to his sister.

Something tugs at my heart—probably my conscience.

It's a terrible thing to have in this situation, where I want the very thing I promised to keep Tessa from. I'm screwed.

My phone vibrates with an incoming text. Victoria.

Did you get a date for tmrw night?

Shit. I was going to ask Tessa to come to the awards dinner tonight, but worried brothers have a way of putting an end to dates.

What are you doing up so late?

Beatrice can't sleep, so neither can I. You didn't answer the ?

I'll get back to you in the morning.

Okay. Night, Barc.

Night, sis.

I understand Miles' feelings about his sister. I'd want to punch a guy if he were after my innocent sister too. It's time to admit one thing to myself: I'm not after Tessa for just sex, though I wish I were making love to her right now under this cloudless night sky.

It's a different kind of physical desire. More an … indescribable pull I feel toward her. Tessa isn't a mere conquest. I want to discover what makes her *her*. In all my years, I've never experienced this feeling with any other woman. I'd always thought it was a fairy tale. Maybe I'm wrong to carry on after her, but I don't want to miss out on the chance if I'm right.

Leaving the terrace, I walk back inside my apartment, pick up the house phone that connects directly to the hotel lines, and press in Tessa's room number.

"Listen, Miles. For the millionth time, I'm sorry for putting you through—"

"Tessa, it's Barclay," I interrupt her.

"Oh thank God." She sighs, and I imagine her collapsing on the bed. "I'm so sorry and need to thank you for everything you did tonight and also apologize for my brother's overreaching ways. He can't understand that I'm not fifteen."

"First, I have a sister too, and might have been no different. And second, you can thank me by saying yes."

"Yes?" she says, like it's a question. At least she trusts me enough to utter the word.

"Good. Now that we have that cleared up, you're going to attend the Warwick Awards with me. Dinner begins at seven. I'll have a car outside the hotel at six thirty. Be prompt. You'll be attending as my plus one, on the request of Don Black. To avoid the press and photos, we aren't officially on a date." I pause, taking a breath. I went into CEO mode with her so easily.

"Wow. Thanks. Of course I'll go with you," she replies. "I wasn't sure I'd ever hear from you again after tonight."

"You think cops with guns will keep me away from you? I want you, Tessa—like I've never wanted a woman before."

"I feel the same about you. Well … but as wanting a guy, not a woman. I think I'll quit while I'm behind." She giggles, and the cheerful sound makes me grin like a silly teenager.

"I promised your brother I'd watch over you, so having you near me seems like the best plan. But tomorrow night, you'll text your family. Let them know you're back at the hotel after the dinner. You just don't need to mention you're with me."

"Yes," she breathes.

"Good night, beautiful."

I pour one more scotch, but this time, I drink it with a smile on my face.

27

Tessa

The phone blares next to me on the nightstand. My hand hits around on the wood until it connects with the offensive machine disturbing my sleep. I don't even open my eyes as I find the receiver and bring it to my ear.

"Hello," I rasp. My throat feels parched—something I don't experience often living in the humid south.

"Good morning, sleepyhead." It's Barclay, and he's way too chipper for this early in the morning. It's like he swallowed a happy pill.

I peek at the clock next to the phone. It's nine, not too early, but I tossed and turned last night after my brother humiliated me. I thought my father quizzing my dates in his full-blown sheriff's uniform with a gun holstered to his belt was bad in high school. Boy, was I wrong. Having the CEO of one of the world's top publishing companies grilled by your brother was to the moon and back worse.

"You must be a morning person," I mumble, tossing the covers off me. I press the speaker option on the phone and pad over to the mini-bar, needing to hydrate from all the drinking last night. I pop open a bottle of water and take a gulp. It tastes like heaven.

"And you apparently aren't." I feel the smile behind his words, and I grin too.

"You've seen one sunrise, you've seen them all," I singsong, then take another swig of water.

"Someday, I'll show you one to change your mind." His voice is gravelly with a hidden meaning. I sit down on the bed by the nightstand, hug my legs to my chest, and smile.

"All talk." I laugh.

"Soon, you'll wake up in my arms with the early morning sun shining on us." His tone is husky and full of promise.

"I hear the weather's supposed to be lovely tomorrow morning."

"I'll keep that in mind," he teases with a chuckle. "Today, I have press with Don. He seldom ventures to New York, so he's booked with every news organization known to man. And thanks to you, Hammond is back in his good graces. I want to keep it that way."

"I look forward to seeing that feisty old man tonight."

"Since I'll be tending to His Majesty today, I've made

some plans for you."

"Oh, you have?" I ask, hesitant.

"You might want to write this down," he orders. I grab the notepad and pen from the desk. "Room service will bring you breakfast in thirty minutes. From noon to three, you'll be pampered at Spa Bellerosé on Fifth Avenue. Facial, massage. Personal yoga session. Whatever you want. I'll have a car at your service. Just introduce yourself to the doorman."

"I've never had anything so extravagant. I can't accept this," I protest. My idea of a spa day is an upgraded pedicure.

"Don't argue. You're already on their book," he says, giving me a gentle reprimand—one he probably uses in the boardroom. "Then, my personal stylist, Gloria Herman, from Saks, will bring several dresses to your hotel room at four. Pick one for tonight. I told her you'd want something in pink and guessed a petite size two. Close?"

"Yes, but ..." I try to stop him, but it's no use. He rolls on with his crazy, spoil-Tessa list. I bite back a smile, hardly believing he's doing all of this for me.

"A hair and makeup stylist should be there by five. Sound okay?" he asks.

"It's too much," I exclaim, but have a feeling nothing I say will change his mind. I feel like a princess, and he's ruining me for all other men.

"One more thing." His tone turns serious. "When I threw you over my shoulder in the lobby last night, someone took a photo of us and it did end up making Page Six of the Post."

"Just great," I say, shaking my head. I bet it was the man with his camera phone.

"I'm sorry, Tessa. But there is a bright side since they only have your backside, not your face, in the photo. The Post labeled you the 'unknown blond woman.' They contacted me, and I declined to give your name, of course."

My muscles tense as an uneasy feeling sweeps over me. Barclay stands out in a crowd, and the focus of attention follows him wherever he goes. He's New York's publishing prince with his dark Armani suit as his coat of armor, and anyone standing near him is a casualty of his celebrity, including this unknown girl from an unknown town in Alabama.

"Try not to worry," he urges me. "I need to run. I'm at CNN. They're interviewing him for a segment. Enjoy your day, Tessa. I can't wait to see you tonight."

"Thank you, Barclay," I say as he ends the call, but it doesn't seem to be enough for all he's done for me. I'm blown away and can hardly process it all.

I fall back against the bed and stretch out my limbs with a huge smile plastered on my face. A facial at a New York spa would've been over the top by itself, but no, I'll be wearing a dress from Saks Fifth Avenue.

I walked by their storefront windows after a stop at Rockefeller Center yesterday and dreamed of strolling into the store someday and buying clothes without a care to the price. And now, Barclay's making them come to me.

But one fact looms over my head like a dark rain cloud: I

still don't have a job. Even the two promising interviews next week aren't a sure thing until an offer is made. In two weeks, I might be back in Monroeville working at Dairy Queen, but for today, I'm getting treated like a queen thanks to Barclay.

I call Maggie and give her the rundown on what happened last night and the day Barclay's planned for me.

"He's so into you, Tessa. Spa, clothes from Saks. Glamming you up for the night." When Maggie runs down the list, it truly blows my mind.

"It's like I'm living a fairy tale. Oh, and one more thing. But you have to keep this vaulted. Promise me?" I ask. "If Miles or my parents find out ..."

"My lips are sealed. *Promise*," she stresses, but doesn't really have to. I'd trust her with anything, even something that would get my brother on a plane to bring me home.

"I made Page Six ... sort of," I confess quietly, still in disbelief. I don't know much about Page Six, but if it's a big deal, Maggie will bring me up to speed.

"What? You're kidding me, right?" she asks, but doesn't give me time to answer. "Wait, I'm checking online for the photo."

I take a deep breath and wait for her to find the photo. I haven't seen it yet either. Once I do, it will seem too real. I'd rather not have it burned into my brain.

"Oh my God. It's the top story. Have you seen it?" she rushes out.

"No," I reply, but she doesn't stop.

"It's a side view of Barclay with you draped over his shoulder. Nice ass shot by the way. She laughs, and I cringe. "It says, 'Barclay Hammond carried a young blond woman over his shoulder through the lobby of the Hammond Hotel. This is the first time he's been spotted with someone since his breakup with longtime girlfriend, Amanda Lake.' First, screw Amanda. Second, I can't believe you're in town for a few days—and boom! You've already landed on New York's most talked about gossip column. It was my goal to make that page in five years tops. I'm in awe."

"It's a nightmare," I whisper, because the fallout could be severe. "If my family finds out, they'll never be okay with me moving here. It's like their worst fears have come true."

"When you land a job next week, and I believe you will, you're going to have to tell them about Barclay. He's crazy for you, and there's no way to keep news about a man like him contained. At least Miles will know who he is, right?"

"Barclay also promised Miles he'd keep an eye out for me."

"Awkward, but will anyone be good enough for you in Miles' eyes?"

"Probably not." I sigh. "I've got to run and get ready."

"It's tough being you," Maggie quips. "Send me a selfie before you leave for the dinner."

"Wish me luck," I say.

"Nah. You've got that in spades. I'll wish that you get f—"

"Goodbye, Maggie."

28

BARCLAY

The attendees for the Warwick Awards arrive in a steady stream. This is my first awards dinner as Hammond's CEO, though I've been the prince in line to the throne for several years. I work the crowd and shake hands with rival publishers. Discuss the changing trends of our markets in the broadest of terms. Always putting a hopeful spin on what lies ahead.

Several of them congratulate me on Don Black's latest hit, telling me he's a shoo-in for book of the year. I graciously tell them it's anyone's guess, but their knowing eyes tell me it'd be a shock if he lost.

One thing's for sure, every time I hear his name, I breathe

a sigh of relief. He decided to stay with Hammond, and I have Tessa to thank for that.

Knowing Tessa should be arriving soon, I excuse myself from the gathering and make my way to the lobby to greet her. Don's holding court at the bar. He has a drink in one hand and an arm wrapped around a brunette, who isn't his wife. *Old flirt.*

My phone buzzes, and I answer.

"What's up?" Tom Rogers, a fellow colleague, and his wife pass by me. I nod and raise my free hand.

"Sorry to bother you on the weekend, Mr. Hammond, but it's rather urgent," my head of marketing, Reece Young, says in a rush, though I can't tell if it's from excitement or concern.

"I'm at the Warwick and it's getting ready to start, so make it quick."

"There's crazy buzz circulating on the street about the person I've set my sights on for millennial marketing. I need to get your okay for an out of the ordinary offer."

"I discussed this with Mrs. Ratner." Usually the exacts for any offer go through my human resource director. She works as a mediator between forces. "I gave my blessing for the title of junior marketing manager and a subsidized apartment. What more do you have in mind? The candidate did just graduate from college."

"It's the blog they started. It has an enviable audience in the millennial marketplace directed toward serious readers. Believe me, we need this person. Here's what I'd like to propose. Seventy-five a year and we buy the rights to the blog with them continuing to grow it under the Hammond brand. Two other houses are looking to ask similar offers this week, but aren't buying the blog. I say we strike first. Lay out the terms and ask for an immediate decision."

Peering out the lobby's door, I spot a blonde goddess with legs for days walking up the steps. "Make the offer, but keep the blog's buy price at twenty-five or less. If anything, it will help them pay off possible student loans. Good luck."

I pocket the phone, and stand in the shadows next to an interior wall, avoiding the reporters and cameras outside. They're not allowed inside, so Tessa and I are safe past the entrance.

My smile grows with every step she takes toward me. Her dress hits mid-thigh with a feather hem showcasing her toned legs. The color is the lightest pink, like a chilled glass of rosé. A single strap around her neck holds up the dress. I bite my lip, imagining how little it would take for her dress to fall to the ground around her stiletto heels. The thought may drive me wild during the dinner.

The dress dips low between her breasts, revealing soft and ample cleavage. My eyes feast on all the exposed skin I can't wait to explore.

The curve of her breasts. Delicate shoulders and neck. An uncovered back my fingers itch to touch.

Her outfit's cut is daring, jaw dropping even, but classy enough for a black tie event. It fits her age, and will turn every head in the room.

Her blond hair is off her shoulders and twisted into a smooth knot, making her appear older, sophisticated, and perfectly formal.

Her azure colored eyes shine with curious excitement as she looks from side to side. She wears a stifled smile, as if she's containing a full-blown grin. God, I want to possess those full pink lips of hers.

A man near the entrance leers at Tessa with greedy eyes, and opens the door for her. When she crosses the threshold, he ogles her from head to toe. *Prick.* It's a call to action, so I step out of the shadows and move toward her.

When Tessa's eyes find mine, a radiant smile lights up her face, leaving me breathless. Her beauty shines so intensely, I feel its warmth.

"You're simply stunning." I greet her, taking one of her hands. I hold it up and spin her around on her heels. She giggles quietly. When the quick twirl reveals all her luminescent skin, I act on impulse—or raging hormones. "Come with me for a minute."

"Where are we going?" She turns a curious eye toward me, tilting her head to the side. I glance over my shoulder as I guide her a few steps away and around a corner.

"Trust me?" She nods, and I point to the closed door in front of us.

"The cloakroom?" she asks with a teasing smile.

"Shush," I whisper, twisting the handle to see if it's locked. It moves in my hand. I'm in luck.

I open the door wide enough for us both to slide inside,

then leave it cracked a few inches so a sliver of light streams in. Aside from a few empty hangers on a rod, the room is bare.

"What are we doing in here?" Tessa asks, but her eager eyes give her away. She wants me as much as I want her.

"I need something from you before we join the others." I lean forward and speak into her ear.

"What's that?" she breathes.

"This." I place my hands on her back. She shivers at my touch, following with a sweet sigh. My fingers trail over her velvety skin, lingering at the simple hook connecting her lone strap. If only we had more time. "Your skin's so smooth and silky."

I bend down and kiss her lips, and she returns it with a passion matching mine. Tessa links her fingers behind my neck, and we are lost in each other. Minutes later, when we both need to draw in a breath, I move my lips down her neck and over the exposed curves of her breasts.

"I want to taste all of you," I say against her skin, and feel her pulse racing like mine.

Dropping to my knee, I bring my hands to the back of her toned legs, and trace the delicate skin behind her knees. Her muscles flex and release in anticipation. With a featherlike touch, I inch up her thighs, finding the lacy edge of her panties. "Has anyone touched you here?"

"No one," she blows out between labored breaths. She gazes down at me with eyes full of desire, but there's a tentativeness in them I can't ignore. My touches, and the promise of more between us, are new and unchartered territory for her.

I rise to my full height, changing our position. Looking down at her, I wonder if this beautiful woman is ready for what I want to do to her and what we can be together. I have to ease her into things, build her confidence. It should be her decision to freely give into the passion and trust me. Let me make her mine. I won't push her from the base of the mountain to the peak in one night.

"I want to be the first. Are you okay with that?" I run my fingers over the curve of her shoulders.

"Yes, please," she begs. "Can we skip the dinner and leave now?"

"If only I could whisk you away, but duty calls. We won't stay a second longer than necessary." I give her a quick kiss on the forehead. "We better get the evening started."

We adjust our clothes and smooth errant hairs, trying to remove the evidence of our quick tryst.

"You look like you've been assaulted by a tube of lipstick." Tessa pulls a tissue from her bag and cleans the lipstick from my face. I left a pink trace on the curve of her breasts with my stained lips, and return the favor, wiping away the mark. My fingers delve below the fabric, desperately wanting to feel what's hidden to my eyes.

Sadly, I pull my hands away. Touching all of her will have to wait—something I need to remind my raging erection. I can't walk into the ballroom full of fellow publishing professionals with tented pants. I try to think of something to distract me, but she's too close for anything other than her to register in my lust-fueled brain. Giving up, I button my suit coat.

Placing my hand on the small of Tessa's back, I guide her into the ballroom, gently rubbing circles across her exposed skin, though it does nothing to help my dick get under control. I've been in complete launch sequence since I saw her exiting the car.

Only a couple people remain standing in the ballroom. Everyone else has already taken their seats. Hammond Publishing has a table front and center since Don's up for the prestigious book of the year award. We make our way through the room and find our place. Don turns in his chair. He looks at Tessa, then me with a sly smile, and gets up to take her hand.

"My dear. You look lovely. Doesn't she, Barclay?" Don eyes me with a knowing air. The old man's baiting me, and I don't like it one damn bit. He brings her hand to his lips and kisses her knuckles.

The same rush I had when I saw Tessa at the bar with my cousin races up my back and elicits a primal urge. I want to pull her away from him, but I steel myself against it. This caveman reaction is something totally foreign to me. I never felt it before meeting her. I take a few deep breaths, trying to get my shit together.

"Hello, Mr. Black," Tessa replies after Don finally drops her hand. I squint one eye at him, and he smiles back at me in amusement. He knows exactly what he's doing.

"Good evening, Don. Enjoying yourself so far?" I ask in a more pointed tone than I should. I know he's all talk and has never strayed from his vows, but still, I want her as mine alone. I wonder what it is about Tessa that makes me feel this way. I'll need to examine these feelings later.

"I am, and will be having an even better one now that Tessa has arrived." Don pulls out the chair seated next to him, and motions toward Tessa. "You're sitting next to me, as I requested."

We settle into our seats, and I introduce Tessa to everyone at the table. I start with my sister, Victoria, and her husband, Danton. She's attending for my mother, who's on the board, but wanted to give the spotlight to her daughter. She hopes Victoria will step into her role soon, leaving her to care for my father as he travels down a dark road with Alzheimer's.

Dinner is served and drinks are refilled. Polite conversation buzzes around the table, and I don't miss the curious stares from my sister and her husband—all aimed at me. Don lays down his claim for Tessa's attention, and monopolizes her with conversation about the current book he's writing. She claims to be his biggest fan, and will make the perfect audience for his big ego. But a happy Don keeps Hammond's bottom line healthy, even if I grind my teeth while trying to ignore how close he's moved toward her.

"I must commend you on your date. I like her," my sister says, pulling me away from Don and Tessa's conversation.

"Tessa's gorgeous and smart, and definitely younger than I'd expect. I'm guessing southern from her accent."

"Yes, Alabama."

"No kidding," Victoria laughs. "Oh, how I wish Mother were here to see you with her. Tessa's the young woman you were eyeing the other night at the Hammond, isn't she?"

"She is." I leave my answer short on purpose. I do hope my mother meets Tessa someday, but I don't want my sister pestering me about it. She has a way of pushing me before I'm ready.

"She's gotten to you, Barclay. In a good way." My sister glances over at Tessa, who's still engrossed in conversation with Don. "In fact, everyone seems captivated by her."

"Seriously, I just met her."

"Doesn't matter. Something tells me this woman is different, apart from her age and background. I can see it in your eyes. The way you look at her."

"And how's that exactly?" I ask, wondering if I'm ready for my sister's answer.

"In awe."

I don't have a direct response, or one I'm ready to say out loud, but I can't deny feeling differently about Tessa too. I was curious to know who she was the moment my eyes landed on her at the restaurant. I wondered if she was waiting for someone else or eating alone. Mostly, I wanted to claw back ten years and be a different, younger version of me.

Then, she appeared in my office the next day wrapped in

Mrs. Mackenzie's coat. She's a temptation I can't seem to resist, even if I still hear her brother telling me to watch out for his sister. It's futile to try to silence his words and my agreement. Instead, I'll treat her like a fucking goddess. Tessa turns my way and gives me a slow, sexy smile. It makes me ache for her. When she ends it with a lip bite, I'm convinced she can live with my decision too.

29

TESSA

The dinner ends with Don winning book of the year, but no one seems shocked, especially those sitting with me at Hammond's table. As we prepare to leave, Don gives me a big, both-arms-around-me hug and uses the closeness to whisper in my ear.

"I've known Barclay for years, and I've never seen him so possessive over a woman. Please don't look over your shoulder, but you should see the look he's giving me now." I fight the urge to turn around and keep my eyes forward. "I don't believe he likes me monopolizing your attention either. Well done, Tessa."

Before I can reply, Barclay's at my side and congratulates

Don one last time, though he shakes his hand without a smile. Then, Barclay guides me out of the ballroom with his hand on the small of my back. His purposeful stride has me walking nearly double-time to keep up with him.

"Don seems very comfortable with you," Barclay clips, pressing his hand harder against me, like he's trying to drive home a point.

"He's a sweet man who shared a lot of things with me," I say, but I can't ignore the irritated tone in Barclay's voice. I look up at him to find him staring out into the lobby with his jaw clenched. Maybe Don's right about how Barclay is with me. A girl can only hope.

"Don's been called a lot of things, Tessa, but sweet isn't one of them," he scoffs. "Forget him. We need to decide on how to handle the press outside. Lawrence, the same driver who drove us to Connecticut, is waiting at the curb for me. I think it's best if you take the car back."

"Okay," I say, and my hope falls to my feet in a silent thud.

I don't want to end up with my face on Page Six tomorrow—my ass and hair was enough, thank you very much—but I don't want the night to end either.

As we walk through the lobby, I stare down at the ground to conceal my disappointment at us parting ways. I imagine he has to attend the after-party Don talked about earlier at the table. But I wanted to be with Barclay tonight, and fight the urge to beg him not to go.

We come to a stop right before the exit to the building. Barclay places a finger under my chin, and I look up at him.

"What's with the pouty face?" he asks, furrowing his brows.

"I wanted to continue the night back at the hotel … with you," I mumble, hoping I don't sound desperate and insecure, even though I am, in all regards.

After meeting everyone around the table, it was clear to me how wide apart our worlds are, and maybe it hit him too. He's experienced and the CEO of a company I'd be happy to have a job sweeping the floors at. It would be a start and more than I have now, which is a big fat nothing.

"Sweet girl," he says with a reassuring smile and a glint in his eyes. It's the same look he had earlier tonight when he kissed me within an inch of my life. "I'll have Victoria drop me by the hotel, and will be knocking on your door in twenty minutes tops."

I exhale the breath I was holding. "You're not going to the party Don mentioned?"

"No, Tessa. Tonight, I have a party with only you." His voice is husky and commanding. "No one else is invited. Just us. How does that sound?"

His words, combined with the hunger in his eyes, makes me feel lightheaded. I reach for his bicep, grabbing a handful of the silken wool.

"Yes, please," I breathe.

Barclay bends forward. The needy look in his eyes intensifies.

"When my stylist helped you choose a dress today, she

left something for you, right?" I nod, remembering the Saks box wrapped securely with a ribbon.

I left it untouched sitting on the counter above the mini-bar. His stylist, Gloria, instructed me not to open it. I'd fiddled with the ribbon, wondering if one quick peek inside was really that big of a deal—I was the kid who snuck around before Christmas trying to locate my presents, after all—but I didn't, for him.

"Go back to the hotel, open it, and get comfortable." He leans even closer as he speaks. His words tickle the skin behind my ear, and I shudder. "Now, get going."

"So bossy," I quip back with a full-blown smile, overjoyed our night isn't ending. He tilts his head toward the door with a mischievous grin, and I walk away, though it's hard to leave his side.

I glimpse over my shoulder and see Victoria approaching him. She looks between Barclay and me like she did a few nights ago at the restaurant, but this time, she smiles at me, and I wave goodbye, hoping to see her again in a less formal setting. I bet she has a few stories to tell about growing up with Barclay.

A man opens the entrance door for me, and I glance down the steps toward the curb. I spot Lawrence standing by the car and head in his direction. I hope he speeds to the hotel, because I can't wait to find out what's in the box.

When I arrive at the hotel, I scurry through the lobby, my heels sliding over the polished marble. Once I make it up to my room, I glance at the box and the mess I left behind getting ready for the dinner. I have no idea which one I should tackle first.

I don't want him to think I'm a slob, so I grab the free plastic bag hotels give for miscellaneous items, like dirty laundry, and set out on a mission. I scoop items up off the bed and floor, filling the bag to the top. Then I throw hangers into the closet, and toss the bag, along with a few clothing items.

I scan the room. It looks lived in, but presentable. Now, for the box. I pull on the ribbon and untie the bow, then remove the top. Tissue paper covers what's inside, secured with a designer seal. I gently tear the seal away and push the paper to the side, revealing a shear ice pink negligée with a matching lace thong. I finger the silk straps of the sexy garment. It's beautiful, but I've never worn anything like this before. Not even to just try on.

My breathing becomes quick and shallow. *"Get comfortable,"* he'd said.

Is that sex speak for get dressed up in lingerie?

When I move the box to the bed, the phone on the nightstand begins to ring. I worry my lip. Could it be Barclay canceling? I take two steps toward the phone and place my hand on the receiver. After a deep breath, I answer it.

"Hello," I say in a shaky voice.

"Tessa," my mother sputters. "I've been trying to get a hold of you all night. How are you, dear? Back in the room for the night?"

"Hi, Mom. Sorry I missed your calls," I say, debating how

much I should tell her about my day, including the dinner with Barclay. "And yes, I'm going to bed soon."

It's not a full-blown lie, more like wishful thinking, and besides, too much information will bring up questions I don't know how to answer yet. It's not like I'm sixteen and missing curfew. I'm a grown woman.

"Is New York everything you thought it would be, dear?" she asks.

"Oh, Mom, you have no idea—" There's a loud knock at my door, and I pause. It's *him*. It has to be him. Panic sets in.

What do I do?

30

TESSA

"What is it, Tessa? Is everything okay?" No one knows me better than my mother, and from over a thousand miles away, she senses something is up. She's right too.

I have a cover model worthy CEO dressed in a bespoke tuxedo with sex on his mind standing at my door. It's not a scenario my mother or I dreamed of when I got on the plane and left Alabama. All I dared to hope for was a decent job— or the prospect of one.

At least I'm not sleeping my way to the top. It's the only solace I have in Barclay not helping me find a job at his company. He must think it would complicate things between us. Plus, there's my lack of experience with guys, let alone older men like him, and it's complicated enough.

"Hold on a second. Someone's at the door." In a hurry to get to Barclay, I can't find the mute button on the phone display.

I lay the receiver down on the nightstand next to the phone and walk to the door, passing by the satiny, sheer negligée sitting in a heap on the bed. Another complication I can't hide. I smooth my dress down over my hips, adjust the halter strap around my neck, and open the door.

My breath leaves me in a rush. Barclay's leaning against the doorframe, one hand in his pocket while he uses the other arm to brace himself. I lost my heels when I arrived back at the room and forgot to put them back on in my haste, so he hovers over me more than usual. He's a massive man, and so massively hot, I might melt into a puddle. I should've told my mother goodbye and that I loved her. His looks are that lethal.

And how did his stubble get even sexier on the ride over to the hotel?

"Hi," I breathe, and it takes quite the effort just to push that one syllable through my lips.

I stand there, staring up at him, holding the door, not fully open. Basically, he can't maneuver around me. There's not enough space.

"Can I come in?" he asks, flashing me a devastating smirk. It'd likely work as a passkey to any woman's room, and I think he knows it too.

"Well, there's a problem ..." I pause, and he raises his brow. "It's my mother."

"Is she here?" He tries to peek around me into the room, but I pull the door tighter toward me.

"Actually, she's on the phone. Waiting." I hold an index finger up to my lips, and his mouth forms a sexy O.

"I'll be as quiet as a mouse," he whispers, crossing his hand over his heart.

"Okay, but please, not a word," I admonish, opening the door wide enough for him to enter.

Barclay tiptoes into the room. It's not a common display for six-foot-something publishing moguls, and I cover my mouth when laughter bubbles up. He lets his fingers linger over the pink satin on the bed and glances at me with dark eyes. I shake my head at him and mouth, *"Later."* He pouts like a little child being told no, which I don't have time for. I push him past the bed, and he sulks over to the window area, sitting down in an upholstered chair paired with a side table.

Giving me the universal finger drag across his mouth, meaning his lips are zipped, I pick up the receiver before my mother calls the front desk asking them to check on me—or worse, tells Miles something's wrong. I sure don't need the police showing up here two nights in a row.

"Sorry, Mother. There was someone from the hotel at the door." Barclay does own the hotel, but I'm stretching the truth, which equals a white lie.

Lying is something I don't do with her—or anyone, for that matter. The only time I feel justified in doing so would be to protect someone's feelings. Honestly, I'm doing something similar now, since my lies will keep her from worrying when I know everything is fine with me. I glance at Barclay, who's smiling deviously. Things are crazy, out-of-my-mind fine.

"You seem out of breath and flustered, Tessa. What did they want?" she asks.

Barclay picks up a book I have sitting on the side table next to him. I forgot all about it in the rush to clean up the room. Big mistake too. He glances down at the cover and looks up at me with a pointed stare that quickly turns into the devil's smile.

He holds the book up for me to see, as if I have no clue what it is, and nods his head approvingly. Opening the book up to the first dog-eared page, he waggles his brows. I have no idea which page it is, but I can only imagine since it's *The 365 Days, 365 Positions Handbook.*

How do I ever recover from this one?

I look away from the sexy smile lighting up Barclay's face as he peruses the book. He keeps peering up at me from the pages and either shaking or nodding his head. A flush spreads across my cheeks. I want to put my mother on hold and rip the book from his hands, but I wonder if he'd let me. He seems to be enjoying it too much.

"Uh, it's uh … it's someone from the hotel doing a nightly turndown service." Another white lie, laced with some truth, because I believe Barclay and I will be under the sheets, or at least on top of them, soon.

"Imagine that. Southern hospitality in a big city like New York." I exhale in relief, but breathe in a lungful of guilt.

I never hide things from my mother. I even told her about the guys pressuring me to have sex in college, knowing they just wanted to claim me as a virginal prize.

"I need to go," I say, more rushed than I should, but Barclay has set down the book and the look in his eyes makes me squirm. It's like he's a tiger ready to pounce ... on me.

"Remember, you promised your grandmother you'd light a candle for your grandfather at Saint Patrick's Cathedral tomorrow."

"I'll go to the ten-fifteen service. The choir sings then."

As we hang up, I can't dismiss how insane it is that I'm discussing church services while sexy lingerie sits on the bed close to the man who may cash in my V-card. But I'm ready ... I think—or more like I should just do it and not think about it. Actually, I'm a freaking emotional mess.

31

TESSA

"My family keeps interrupting us." Sitting on the edge of the bed, I place the receiver in its cradle, exhaling a big sigh. "They mean well, though."

"It was messing with my conscience, but I'm over that after thumbing through your latest read." Barclay places my sex handbook back down on the table and tilts his head to the side. He gives me a quizzical look, and a flicker of a smile passes over his face. "Did you find that book at the Monroeville Library?"

"Ha. Ha." I fake a laugh at the thought of this book on any shelf in my hometown. I've hidden it under my bed since I returned back home from graduating college and snuck it into my suitcase. "My best friend Maggie gave it to me for research purposes. Besides, my mother's the town librarian. If she put something like that on the shelves, it would be her last day working there."

"Well, your eagerness completely disarms me, but there's so much more you need to experience before you get to those positions. Foreplay for one, and the kind I'm talking about isn't something you can learn from the pages of a book. It takes practice."

Barclay licks his lips and trails his eyes over my body, making me shift. His smoldering stare awakens an unfamiliar feeling low in my belly. If anyone else gave me this kind of look in the confines of a hotel room, I would run out the door, screaming for help. With Barclay, I want to fling myself into his arms and get lost in his kisses and touch.

"I can't stop thinking about the things I want to do to you, Tessa. It would blow your sweet mind. What do you want? Tell me," he gravels in a husky voice.

"I want you, Barclay. Show me all the things. Please," I beg, like a starving pauper who hasn't had a meal in days.

Barclay pushes up from the chair, standing tall and stately, adorned in formal attire. His large presence overwhelms the room—and me. My body hums in a delicate balance of nerves and need. Hiding my silly fear, I fold my trembling hands in my lap while my heart races away. I thought I'd be braver than this when the time came to be with someone, but I'm scared shitless.

He takes off his black tuxedo jacket, revealing a fitted

dress shirt that sinfully molds to his sculpted muscles. I swallow hard and lick my lips. After carefully laying his jacket down on the chair, he stalks toward me in a couple long strides.

When Barclay stops in front of me, I lift my chin to gaze up at his handsome face. A cocky smile pulls at the corner of his lips. Watching in heated anticipation, his long fingers tug at his black bowtie, releasing the knot and letting the loose ends lie against his crisp white shirt. Next, he frees the gold cuff links from his starched cuffed sleeves, placing them down on the nightstand with a clink. When he untucks the shirttails from his black pants, I realize he's undressing himself. In. My. Room.

Does he want me to do the same thing?

"Where has the young woman who reads scandalous books gone? You're all wide-eyed and timid now." Barclay gently brushes my cheek with his finger, and I lean into his reassuring touch. "Your mind's spinning away behind those gorgeous blue eyes."

"The truth is …" I pause, and glance away, trying to build up the courage to speak what's in my heart. After a beat, I return to his darkened gaze once again. "I've been waiting for years to have a moment like this, yet I have no idea what to do or what you want. I thought reading books like that would make me brave, but I didn't even change into the lingerie you bought me. Basically, I have no game. I must be a big disappointment."

"Sweet, beautiful girl." Barclay sits down beside me on the

bed, taking my hand in his large one. "Take a deep breath and trust me. Can you do that?"

"Yes. Yes, I will." I fill my lungs and exhale slowly, feeling more relaxed already. He nods in approval.

"Unbutton my shirt, Tessa." His lips brush over my knuckles in the sweetest touch before he releases them.

After another deep breath and an internal pep talk, my fumbling fingers move from button to button, undoing them. Finally, the edges of his shirt are open wide, revealing defined ridges and golden skin. He's all man and muscle, and more gorgeous than I could have imagined.

Barclay encircles one of my hands and lays it against his chest over his heart. He's warm and solid. I feel the steady beat under my palm.

In tentative motions, I rub my fingers over the manly scattering of hair that starts just above his breastbone. It narrows down in a straight line, disappearing under the waistband of his pants. His breathing picks up, and he utters a soft moan, making me emboldened knowing my touch is having an effect on him. I look up into his hooded gaze.

"There's something I've been dying to do all night." He sweeps my hair to the side, and with a ghost of a touch, kisses along the top of my shoulder, trailing to the back of my neck. I can't stop from shivering as my skin ignites with goose bumps. His lips graze the area behind my ear as his fingers toy with the hook of my halter strap. "May I undo your dress?"

"Yes," I whisper, holding a breath. I have nothing on

underneath except delicate silk lace panties, so I'll be exposed with one flick of his wrist.

When he releases the hook, gravity pulls my dress downward. I try to catch it before it falls, but Barclay encircles my wrists, stopping them midair. I feel the dress fall into my lap and close my eyes tightly, hiding myself away.

"Be brave, sweet girl, and open your eyes," he says, trying to soothe away my fears. "You're beautiful. Perfect."

I peek through my lashes to find him drinking in every inch of me, from my lips to my hard nipples. When our eyes meet, his heated gaze helps to melt away my worries. I can tell he wants me, desires me, and most importantly, understands me in this moment. He's the perfect man to help me push past my insecurities.

"Thanks for being so patient with me. I want this. Us," I confess, gesturing between us.

"Tonight, we'll get to know each other's bodies." He drags a lone finger down my spine, and I sigh. "Put the thought of sex out of your mind for now. Relax and enjoy what I'm going to do to you."

"I can do that." The idea of becoming comfortable with him touching me, and me touching him, takes the pressure off performing or understanding something I have yet to experience.

"Have you been with an undressed man before?" he asks me. I shake my head. "Well, that's a good place to start."

He stands up next to me and takes off his shirt, then follows with his shoes, pants, and socks. My heart stops. The only things left are skintight black boxer briefs and a sexy smirk.

Jesus help me, I can't seem to catch my breath. Glancing over him, I try not to stare too long on that *one* spot, but it's no use. He's hard and huge, barely contained in his underwear. Mercy, it's the first time I've seen a penis up close and in person. I want to reach out and touch it. Give it a stroke with my fingers and see if it's real. Instead, I look up at him, sinking my teeth into my lower lip until it hurts. The pain lets me know I'm not dreaming. Barclay and his large member are real.

32

"Lay your head on the pillows," I command, and Tessa obeys in quick measure. Her hair billows around her face, shimmering in the dim lights.

She lies on the bed like an ethereal goddess—the kind men fought wars over, killed, and died for. Yet she doesn't have a clue what she does to me, how I'd love to fully claim her like a chest-pounding Viking until she moans my name.

I push those thoughts aside and climb up next to her on the bed, easing the pink dress down her slender legs, then tossing it to the floor. Tessa gazes up at me shyly, like she's asking me if I approve of what I see. Hell yes I do.

Blond hair of an angel, and a body so sinful, even the devil would blush. Long toned legs, curved hips leading to a small waist, full breasts with a shade of pink that matches her pouty lips.

"You're perfection," I say with a sense of awe. She exhales the breath she's holding and smiles back at me. What's happening between us is brand new for her, and my encouragement builds her confidence.

I glance down at the miniscule lace between her legs. It's a sheer veil letting me see enough to know she's bare underneath. It's not what I expected from a virgin, but neither was the sex handbook.

Positioned at the end of the bed, I wrap my hands around her slim calves. Gently parting her legs, I place one on each side of me, making her open and vulnerable to me. Her panties are wet at the center, and I lick my lips, imagining her sweet taste.

In slow brushes, I caress the inside of her calves, testing the waters for a reaction. She squirms under my fingertips and gazes up at me with pleading eyes.

"You like that?" I ask with a smirk, knowing full well she's going out of her mind with anticipation.

"Please, don't stop," she begs, holding the white bedding tight in her fists.

I continue a path up the inside of her thighs, across the silky lace, until I have the weight of her breasts in my hands. They're firm, full, and real, her nipples peaked, ready for my touch. My thumbs pass over the tight center in a quick back and forth graze. She hums in appreciation.

"Please, Barclay. Please." I glance up to find her eyes closed, and her face twisted somewhere between pleasure and pain. Basically, she's a needy mess, and I love it.

"Look at me, Tessa." Her lashes flutter until she gazes up at me, her baby blues clouded with desire. "What do you want?"

"More. I need more."

"Do you need me to take care of that ache?" My hands slide down her side, toying with the lace of her panties.

"Yes, please," she breathes.

Lowering my body between her thighs, I press my boxer-clad erection against her sex. After a deep breath, I begin to swivel my hips as I thrust forward. Tessa presses herself against me, giving us both more friction. She's so wet and slick.

I smile down at her, and she answers me back with a lazy grin. Ready to give her even more, I take a nipple into my mouth, flick it for a while with my tongue, then suck it between my lips. She grabs on to my back for dear life and lets out the sweetest moan.

"Oh my God," Tessa cries, arching her back, then weaving her fingers through my hair. "I had no idea it could be like this. Everything you're doing is magical." I hold off a laugh and smile, loving her innocent dirty talk.

"No one's ever told me I'm magical before," I whisper in her ear. "Thanks."

"You are. Do that flicking thing with your tongue again." This time, I chuckle, because that tongue move is nothing compared to the one I'd like to do somewhere else.

"So bossy," I tsk.

Unexpectedly, she wraps her legs tight around my waist, and I realize we've gone past the taking-it-slow-part straight into teenage dry humping, and I'm all game. Hell, I can't remember the last time I came in my boxers, maybe junior year at boarding school.

In all fairness to Tessa, she missed this rite of passage, and needs one full-fledged dry hump before she experiences the real thing. It's kind of like warming up in the batter's box. After a good practice swing, she'll be ready to take the real pitch.

"Put your hands over your head." She lifts her arms up and lies them on top of the pillows, causing her breasts to press up into me. Pouty lips and perky boobs—her body's a wet dream centerfold.

Moving my hand up, I grasp both of hers in mine and press them into the pillows.

"Okay with that?" I ask, looking into her eyes. She nods and bites her lip tentatively, yet wants more.

Needing to feel even more of her, I wrap my free arm under her knee and place her leg in the crook of my elbow. Adjusting to the new position, I start to push and thrust forward harder, keeping the spin of my hips.

"Oh my God," she mutters after a few passes, her eyes closed so snug, I can hardly make out anything but her long lashes. "I'm going to die."

Me too. "Oh, sweet girl. I've got you."

I thrust, swivel, push on repeat, feeling my own orgasm begin to claw at me. I suck her nipple into my mouth and bite down on it harder than before. Her legs begin to shake, and I don't let up one damn bit.

"Ohmyohmyohmy. Ahhhhh," she mumbles, chasing her orgasm until she starts to relax in my arms.

When she looks up at me in complete bliss, something unspoken passes between us. It's deep, definitely beyond the moment of lust, and like nothing I've ever experienced before with a woman. And it's her breathy sounds, and the scent of her sex floating in the air, that push me over a cliff like I'm free-falling.

"*Fuck,*" I call out in a long, loud groan after a couple more thrusts, squeezing my eyes shut. I collapse beside Tessa and try to catch my breath.

Holy shit. *What the hell was that?*

I wasn't even inside her. I open my eyes to find Tessa staring right back at me, searching my face. She's so beautiful in her sweet afterglow. I give her a reassuring smile and kiss the tip of her nose. Her eyes fill with happiness.

"Jesus, Tessa," I pant. "That wasn't your first time, was it?"

"Well, I thought I'd had one before, but now I'm not so sure." She stretches her body out on the bed and gives me a satisfied smile. "That was mind-blowing, out of this world, and beyond anything I ever could've imagined. Can we do it again, please?" She pouts her lips and bats her eyelashes as if I need convincing.

"Absolutely. I plan on keeping you around. You're great for my ego." I trail my hand down her neck and over her breasts.

"I get why people could go blind from having them now," she says in a matter of fact way. I lift an eyebrow at her, surprised by this off the wall comment.

"Who told you something crazy like that?"

"Sister Mary Agnes."

"Sweetheart, I'm pretty sure that was a guilt tactic."

"Well, she can suck it. Nothing's going to rain on my orgasm parade." In a fit of giggles, Tessa curls into me, but I have a mess in my boxers. I forgot how awkward the teen years were.

"I need a shower. Care to join me?" I get out of bed, and extend my hand toward her. Tessa scrunches one shoulder up and tilts her head. The blush across her cheeks gives me my answer. "Okay, getting naked together can wait. For now."

I bend over, kissing her on the forehead. "Get comfortable. I'll be right back." She sighs.

After my shower, I find Tessa fast asleep, the covers drawn up to her chin. She barely looks over eighteen, and a pang of something twists in my gut. Probably guilt. Sister Mary Agnes would be proud, but frankly, I don't give a shit.

Before I slide in next to Sleeping Beauty, I text room

service and order Pop-Tarts and coffee for two. I instruct them to deliver the food to Tessa's room at eight a.m.

Eating junk food in bed while watching junk TV is my Sunday morning tradition. It's a welcome escape from the pressure I face at Hammond again on Mondays. I hope she likes the cherry-flavored ones. They're my favorite.

33

The clock reads four fifty-five a.m. and I'm wide-awake. I went to bed at ten, thinking I'd be alert and ready for my two interviews this afternoon. *But no.* My overactive mind kept me up most of the night, focusing on all kinds of scenarios.

Like ...

What if I don't get a job? Then I'll have to leave New York City and Barclay behind. *Does Barclay really like me?* He did invite me out to dinner tonight, so that's a plus in my column. *What if I do get a job?* An apartment on my entry-level salary will be difficult to find.

Question after question spun in my head. Poets call it the dark night of the soul. Others, insomnia. *Me?* A typical

Monday when everything you've hoped for is on the line. At least the weekend with Barclay was wonderful beyond words. The lingering high will carry me through the day.

At six o'clock, I drag myself out of bed to get ready. I pin my hair up in a French twist and add a minimal amount of makeup. The women here don't seem to get all glammed up like those outrageous ladies on the housewives' show.

Aiming for a polished look, I pick a black skirt with subtle pink piping around the hem and pair it with a pink collared blouse that fits to form. The long sleeves button at the wrist, giving it a professional flare. After slipping on my comfortable black pumps, my eyes glance over to the black glasses Maggie bought me to wear during the interviews. The glasses are the fake non-prescription kind, but give me a definite librarian vibe. Maggie said it would make me appear serious and more accomplished.

I push the frames over my nose and give myself a once over in the mirror, turning my head from side to side. I look older by a few years, more sophisticated even. Maybe she's right. After all, I'm trying to nail a job in publishing. Looking more like a bookworm certainly can't hurt.

Right before I'm ready to start out for coffee, there's a knock at my door. My heart skips a beat, hoping it might be Barclay before he heads to the office for the day.

I hurry to the door, opening it to find a room service cart and a hotel attendant. She greets me with a big smile.

"Good morning, Miss Holly. I have breakfast for you, courtesy of Mr. Hammond."

"Wow. Thank you."

There's a pot of coffee along with several silver lidded plates. It reminds me of the breakfast Barclay ordered yesterday morning for us. But underneath the fancy spread were Pop-Tarts. I giggle remembering my shock when he picked up the silver tops.

We sat against the headboard and used pillows for our trays like a makeshift picnic. Pop-Tart sprinkles spread all over the covers, but we didn't care as we watched *Seinfeld* and had a sugar rush.

After my last bite, I turned to him, his eyes filled with laughter, and he leaned over and licked away the cherry filling stuck to the side of my mouth. I'd left the jelly smudge there on purpose, hoping for a kiss, and it had worked.

I move out of the way as the woman rolls the cart into the room, placing the tray on the desk near the window. As she passes by, I notice a medium-sized box wrapped with a pink ribbon next to the condiments.

She refuses the tip I offer, telling me she's under orders to accept nothing from me. I roll my eyes and smile knowing Barclay's behind it. He treats me like a princess, and honestly, this last week in New York City has felt like a fairy tale.

After she removes the cart and closes the door, I rush to the tray to see what's in the box. There's an envelope attached, so I open it first and find a handwritten note inside.

Dear Tessa,

Since I was unable to spend all of Sunday with you, I bought you something from Yankee Stadium. Lucas says hello. He also asked for your friend Maggie's number after I told him she was moving here too. Because she will, since I'm not letting you go.

We have reservations tonight at Mr. Chow's if you're still okay with outing our relationship. I know I am. After dinner, let's head back to my penthouse for the night. See what comes up. ;)

And wear something pink. It's now my second favorite color. The first one is the blue color of your eyes.

See you tonight, sweet girl.

Yours,

Barclay

I place the card over my heart and smile like a lovesick loon. I seriously think I've fallen for this beautiful man. *What woman wouldn't?* I remove the ribbon from the box and lift off the top. Inside, there's a pink Yankee ball cap. I pick it up and laugh, imagining manly, six-foot-something Barclay Hammond buying such a girlie souvenir. It tells me one major thing: he likes me too.

Deciding an impersonal one-line thank you text just won't do, I call him. I need to hear his voice before I set out on my big day.

"Good morning," he says in a sexy, slurred tone. Two words from him, and my panties are wet.

"Morning," I reply, a bit too bubbly, but I can't help it. "Thanks for the breakfast, and I love the ball cap."

"You're more than welcome. I need to take you to a home game so you can wear it. I also upgraded your breakfast." I lift the silver lids, revealing a delicious looking cheese omelet and buttery croissants. One even might be chocolate.

"It looks divine. Thank you. Though, I loved eating Pop-Tarts in bed with you yesterday." I pour myself some coffee and watch steam rise from the cup.

"I think you can count on a repeat."

"I hope so."

"Listen, I need to leave for the office, though I'd rather talk to you. I have back-to-back staff meetings all morning. Another reason to hate Mondays."

"Oh, sure. I understand."

"Good luck with your interviews this afternoon. I'm sure you're going to dazzle them, just like you did me." *I dazzled a publishing mogul?* The thought makes me blush and gives me courage at the same time.

"Thanks, Barclay." It's exactly what I need to hear before I walk out the door.

"Knock 'em dead, sweet girl. See you tonight," he says, ending our call.

As soon as I set the cordless receiver on its cradle, the phone rings, and I jump.

"Hello?" I ask, uncertain if it's Barclay again or possibly my mother.

"Is this Contessa Holly?" an unfamiliar woman asks.

"It is," I respond hesitantly.

"Oh, thank goodness I finally reached you!" exclaims the woman, her voice rushed. She takes a quick breath. "I've been trying to get a hold of you all weekend. Pardon me, I'll slow down. I'm Reece Young, marketing director for Hammond Press. I'd like for you to come in for an interview this morning."

The world stands still as I process what she said. Hammond Press. Interview. This morning.

I'm totally confused, though. Barclay just hung up with me on the phone, wishing me luck on my interview with another company, yet an executive from Hammond is calling me.

"Um, yes, of course." Thoughts whirl in my head, but I have to say yes.

Still, I can't help but wonder, is Barclay behind this phone call? Surely he would've mentioned it to me. He does like to surprise me, though this would be an epic one. I have to text him. It doesn't add up.

"Great," she declares. "As soon as we saw your résumé, we've been emailing you for an interview, but Helen Ratner, our human resource director, said there's been no reply and there wasn't a phone number listed on the paperwork. Finally, Mrs. Ratner spoke with Trevor Spears our CFO. He told her you were staying at the Hammond, basically in our own backyard."

"I haven't seen anything from Hammond Press on my email account. Maybe it went to my spam folder?" Could I have missed their emails? It doesn't seem possible, but then again, I've been distracted by the hottest man in New York City.

"Possibly," she says. "Can you be here at nine o'clock?"

"Sure." I adjust the fake glasses on my nose with shaky fingers. She seems to be pushing me to come in as soon as possible. I wonder what the rush is.

"I'll leave your name with security at the front desk. We're doing things a bit different with you. I'll meet with you first, then you'll talk to Mrs. Ratner and go over the process."

The process? It sounds more like my foot will be under a desk soon, not just inside the door.

"Thanks, Mrs. Young," I say, feeling like I'm dreaming.

"Looking forward to it. Oh, and security will give you the details on where to go. See you soon."

I'm frozen in place, shocked by her enthusiasm and the special treatment for me. She's the director for all of Hammond's imprints, and I'm a lowly college graduate without much to offer the company. It doesn't make much sense that she would want me so badly she breaks protocol.

Well, at least I know Barclay had nothing to do this interview, and is likely in the dark too, making it even more imperative I reach out to him.

I text Barclay, wanting him to know where I'm headed before I walk into Hammond Press. It would be beyond awkward if I ran into him once I'm there.

Please call me as soon as you can. It's important.

Forget eating now. My appetite is gone. I pace around the room for a few minutes, knowing I need to leave the hotel soon to make the interview by nine. Finally, I see the bubbling dots beside my text. I wait.

Can't call. Tied up in a budget meeting.

Talking to him will have to wait. Dammit.

I grab my bag, smooth back my hair, and leave for my interview. But something feels off. I should be ecstatic about getting the red carpet treatment, instead there's a weight on my chest like a warning. I could be walking into the job of my dreams—or a nightmare since Barclay never made an effort to help me at Hammond and I don't know why.

34

This time, I walk into the lobby of Hammond Press with both eyes wide open to avoid another coffee mishap. I approach the front desk and the security guard smiles at me. It's the same one who was on duty when I was doused with four javas.

"Hello, again, miss," he says. "How can I help you?"

"I'm here for a nine o'clock interview with Reece Young. My name's—"

"Contessa Holly," he interrupts. "I have instructions here for you. They're a piece of cake. Push the top floor on the elevator panel. Ms. Young's office is a right turn off the elevator and down the last hallway. Her nameplate is on the door. Good luck."

"Thanks," I reply, appreciating his good wishes.

After being here last week, I know the way to the elevator bank and find one waiting open for me. This has to be a good sign. I hop inside and press the button to the top floor.

I follow the guard's instructions to Ms. Young's office and stand in front of a slightly ajar door. Peeking through the small opening, I see a brunette sitting at a desk typing away on a computer. Behind her is a closed door. I'm guessing the woman is Ms. Young's assistant.

I knock on the door, and it opens wider. The woman glances up from her computer screen and gives me a welcoming smile.

"Please, come in." She stands up from her desk, waving me inside, and I enter the office. "You must be Miss Holly. I'm Margaret Lee, Ms. Young's assistant. We've been waiting for you. Can I get you coffee or tea? Maybe water? How about a pastry? They're fresh from the bakery across the street. I bought them myself."

"I'm fine, really. Thank you so much for offering." Her greeting seems overly eager, making me feel like a rock star entering a Green Room backstage.

This kind of attention is way over the top. It makes me wonder again about Barclay's involvement.

"Let me tell Ms. Young you're here." She starts to turn toward the closed door behind her, but stops herself. "By the way, I love your blog. Shakespurr's my favorite. It's so exciting to meet you."

"Thanks," I say in complete shock. She spins around to enter Ms. Young's office and disappears from view. I believe they have me confused with someone else, like literary legends Don Black or Steven Queen.

When Margaret reappears, Ms. Young is walking right behind her. "*Contessa.* Welcome to Hammond," Ms. Young says, her voice ringing with excitement. She strides toward me, hand outstretched. "It's so great to have you here at Hammond," she says as we shake hands.

"I'm so happy to be here." She's a tall, classical beauty with shiny brown hair that falls to her shoulders. Her bright eyes show a keen intelligence, and like everyone in Manhattan, she's gilded in black from head to toe, perfecting the title of senior executive.

"Let's get started. We have a lot to cover and little time." She hustles me into her office, and I follow, confused by everything that's happened, from the rush and press to get me interviewed and the way I've been greeted.

"Please, have a seat." Ms. Young gestures to the empty chairs in front of her desk and sits in a leather one behind it. After I'm seated, she begins. "Do you have any idea what kind of a publishing buzz you've created in this city's marketing departments?"

I scrunch my brows, unsure how to answer her question. "I don't understand what you mean."

"Here's the deal. Shakespurr brings all the millennials to

the shelf. Every time the cat posts a review for a Hammond book, our sales dramatically spike in the twenty-something demographic. Even if the review is less than stellar. You're reaching and moving a segment with your blog that is illusive to us."

"Really? I had no idea my blog was making such an impact ... or being watched here in New York City." I swear, my eyes have to be as round as saucers. I truly can't believe what I'm hearing.

"You have been, and we'd like you to continue doing great things here at Hammond. You've scheduled other interviews, correct?" I nod my head. "That's what I've heard on the street. We want to make you an offer you can't refuse. We need your help to build our millennial audience."

"What do you have in mind?" I ask, sitting on the edge of my seat. All those mock interviews I practiced with Maggie sure didn't go this way. Ms. Young is practically begging me to come work here. *Mind blown.*

"First, we'd like to buy the rights to Shakespurr for twenty-five thousand."

"As in dollars?" I mutter, shell-shocked.

"Yes, only America's finest currency here." She laughs, and I try not to cry. It's like winning the interview lottery. "You'd still be in control of the content, and we'll throw marketing dollars behind it too. Your official title is junior marketing manager with seventy-five thousand as a base salary."

She pauses for a beat, giving me a second to let it all sink in, but it doesn't at all. I'm having an out of body experience, like she's talking to someone else and I'm eavesdropping.

"And since you're moving here from out of state, there's a furnished, subsidized apartment in the Hammond Hotel. The top ten floors are executive rentals, and there's one available now. Perfect timing."

Wait! What? It feels like my wildest dreams are coming true, or someone is playing a horrible joke on me.

"What you're offering me is a substantial package, especially since I just graduated from college. Before I accept it, I have a question, if I may."

"Of course. Ask away."

"Mr. Hammond." I take a breath and decide not to beat around the bush. I don't think it will curb her enthusiasm if I pry just a touch. "What was his part in your decision? I'm curious how such a generous offer came to be."

My stomach twists in anticipation. Her answer will determine my future here at Hammond Press.

"Well, it's been a whirlwind," she says with a crooked smile. "After viewing your résumé, I knew we needed you on board. The entire marketing department talks about your blog daily. Mostly wondering how you do it. Mr. Hammond knows I've been working on the millennial outreach for our imprints, so this was a no-brainer. He approved all the points in your offer."

"So, you mentioned me to him first." She nods. "Has he actually seen my résumé, and does he know me by name?"

"I've been working here for fifteen years. He trusted me

and approved your résumé unseen." She looks up toward the ceiling in thought. "As a matter of fact, I don't believe I even told him your name."

When I exhale, a load lifts from my shoulders. I received this outlandish offer on my own. I feel like jumping out of my seat and fist pumping the air, but I don't think Ms. Young would appreciate it.

After a couple deep breaths, my need to freak out subsides to a controllable level.

"My mind's made up." I beam from ear to ear. "Thanks so much for this amazing opportunity. I will do my best to be a valuable asset here at Hammond. I'll be honest, I can't really believe it, though."

"I was in your shoes many years ago. Fresh out of college." Ms. Young stares at an imaginary spot behind me, reliving memories. "Rarely do I meet a young person who has created something we need. Usually they need us. I feel this is just the beginning for you."

"Thanks for your confidence in me." I hope she's right too.

Ms. Young leads me to an office down the hall from hers belonging to Helen Ratner, head of HR. The company has paperwork for me to fill out before I become official.

"Just formalities at this point," Ms. Young says.

A thought tugs at me. I need to let Barclay know what's happening on his very floor. I don't know how he'll take this surprise. I should've told him about Trevor passing my résumé on to Mrs. Ratner, but it seemed like such a long shot at the time. And it's not like I had notice.

While Mrs. Ratner gathers and shuffles through papers, I fire off a quick text to Barclay.

I need to talk to you asap.

I stare at the phone in my lap, praying to see activity on his side, but there's nothing. The screen fades to black, and I refresh it. Waiting. Hoping.

I begin filling out the basic forms for employment. Background check, detailed personal information, and a non-disclosure form pertaining to company campaigns and authors' future works. I'll take home the health and savings plans paperwork and bring them back tomorrow. I guess this is my first official day on the job. It was like I was hired before I walked into the building.

After I finish with all the forms, I check my phone. Still, nothing from Barclay. Not even an acknowledgement he received my text. He said he'd be covered up with meetings today, but it doesn't feel right. I wish he knew I was the one Ms. Young wanted for this position.

How will he react when he finds out it's me?

"All the forms look good." I settle back in my chair across the desk from Mrs. Ratner. Her gaze scans over my face, appraising me in an unnerving sort of way. She makes a "hmmm-hmmm" sound before speaking again. "You're single, right?"

I show her my left hand and wiggle my fingers. "No ring." This earns me a slight smile from her.

But am I really single? Would Barclay like the way I answered her question?

"It's best I explain Hammond Press' stance on inner office relationships." Mrs. Ratner drops her voice, conveying the seriousness of her next words. "If you want to date someone here at Hammond, they have to be on the same level as you. Your equal. No one can date another person they have authority over. In other words, stay out of your chain of command. Maybe find a nice guy in accounting. He'll be on the other side of the company's organizational chart too. That'd be safe for you."

She points a long, thin finger at the paper in front of me, her nail landing on accounting. She trails a path up, and I don't miss the executive at the top of the pile: Barclay Hammond.

"How long has this policy been in place? The no dating a superior one?" I feel nauseous at this point in the conversation, because the rules are clear. I can't date Barclay—ever. All the roads lead to him.

"The board of directors recently set forth the rules, bringing Hammond up to date with harassment issues in the workplace climate."

I reach up and touch my lips, remembering Barclay's kiss goodbye yesterday morning. *Would it be my last?*

35

BARCLAY

"Trevor, compile last month's revenue for all fiction and non-fiction new releases. Have them on my desk by tomorrow at noon," I order my cousin, giving him a don't-fuck-with-me stare across the conference table.

Thankfully, the meeting is over, because staying professional is near impossible knowing how Trevor treated Tessa last week. I wanted to reach over the table and punch that smirk off his slimy face. The jerk knows how to get under my skin.

Running late for my next meeting, I leave the room and start walking down the hallway. Trevor catches up with me, but I pretend he doesn't exist.

"Have you heard about the new junior marketing hire?" he asks, but I keep ignoring him. My jaw tightens when he doesn't get the message that I have nothing to say.

"She's a sweet southern belle," he continues in a teasing tone. I stop at the boardroom door leading to my next meeting, and unfortunately, he does too. "You'll get to meet her now. She's just behind that door."

"What's your problem, man?" I turn to face him, and a sickening smile spreads across his face.

"I don't have a problem, but you're about to." He cackles like a crazy person, walking away from me without another word. He's totally lost it this time.

I enter the room and find my marketing director, Reece Young, at the head of the table. "Sorry to be late. Accounting's conference ran longer than usual. What did I miss?"

"We have some exciting news," Reece says, standing up and moving around the back of the table. She stops behind the chair of a blonde wearing glasses. Shaking my head, I do a double-take and blink, not understanding what I'm seeing in front of me. "I'd like you to meet Contessa Holly. Our new junior marketing manager."

Reece smiles brightly, as pleased as punch. Me? I feel like I've been punched in the gut. And *"Contessa?"* She looks ghostly pale.

"Tessa?" Her name spills out of my mouth before I can stop it, but deep down, I know it's her. She's wearing pink, and a grave expression, feeling the weight of the moment just like me.

"You two know each other?" Reece asks, glancing back and forth between Tessa and me. Her eyes narrow, assessing us, then there's a flash of curiosity. The tension in the air thickens, pressing against my lungs. I tug at my collar.

How the hell do I answer Reece's question?

I can't tell her I stayed the night in Tessa's room and planned to know her in the biblical sense this evening after dinner. The thought of her lying on my bed, ready and waiting for me to make her mine, helped me push through this morning's dull meetings. Now, she's a forbidden fruit I'll never be able to taste.

"Um, we met at the hotel. In the restaurant." Tessa saves me with a reply we can work with, hopefully removing any suspicious thought from Reece's mind. What a fucked-up mess.

"That's right." I force a smile, trying to make our meeting seem inconsequential, which is a boldface lie. The second my eyes connected with Tessa's, my life pivoted into the before and after I found *her*.

Dammit. We're royally fucked. The rules are clear. I'm the king of the company. Everyone is off limits to me.

Somehow, I take my seat at the other end of the board-room table, running my fingers through my hair. My gaze stays on Tessa, still not fully believing she's here in this room.

Her blond hair is twisted on top of her head, and she spins an escaped lock around her slender finger. A profound sadness is etched across her face, making my chest ache.

When her eyes cloud, she looks down at the table, closing them. I fight the urge to drag her out of the room and into my office.

I need to know how this happened. *Has she been using me or my name this entire time to get a job?* The thought doesn't ring true to the Tessa I know, but I've been played many times in my thirty-seven years.

"Miss Holly was sharing a dynamic marketing idea with us," Reece says. "I'm very impressed."

I glance around the table. Everyone but Tessa has a hopeful smile on their face. They're all thrilled to have her here.

At this point, the initial shock is wearing off, simmering into anger. I'm angry with Tessa for keeping this from me. I'm angry with myself for falling for her. But mostly, I'm furious I'll never have her in my arms again, where I thought she belonged.

"Well, Miss Holly, it appears you've dazzled everyone. Tell me how you plan to help us grab twenty-somethings for Hammond Press. I'm dying to know," I clip, a harsh edge to my voice.

Across the length of the boardroom table, Reece tilts her head, raising a defined brow at me. I ignore her and turn my focus back to Tessa.

"Well, I have an idea that still needs flushing out." She wipes her eyes and clears her throat. *Fuck, she's crying.*

"Are you okay, Miss Holly?" Reece asks, pushing a box of tissues toward her.

"Thank you," Tessa says, dabbing her eyes. "Allergies. Not used to the New York City air yet."

Again, Reece scrutinizes the two of us. She's smart, intuitive, and dangerous to me at this point. I need to take my tone down and act like Tessa is a normal new hire—not the woman I've fallen for who possibly deceived me.

"Take your time," I say, more reserved and patient. Tessa regards me and mouths two powerful words, *"I'm sorry." But for what?*

After composing herself, Tessa begins.

"Right now, Shakespurr has one hundred thousand plus followers on Instagram. We can build buzz off it. Connect it to my blog and change the name to Hamming It Up. Then ask the audience to send photos of themselves reading Hammond books.

"For instance, we could post a photo of Don Black's book being read at a Paris café or Steven Queen's at Buckingham palace. The readers will love the attention and tag. Win. Win." Tessa sits back in her chair, her shoulders slumping, as if she has nothing else to give.

I can't deny I'm impressed with her idea and the fact that she has so many built-in followers. Most importantly, I didn't have any clue she was behind the Shakespurr blog Don referred to and even named his cat after. It's another secret she kept from me. *How many more are there?*

"Promising," I say, summing up her presentation with muted enthusiasm.

"You're kidding, right?" Reece cuts in, throwing her hands

up in frustration. "Mr. Hammond, I'm having her work on this concept this afternoon. Your approval or not."

"Have at it. Anything else I need to know?" I ask, waving a hand in a roundabout motion, signaling it's time to move the agenda on from the new junior executive.

I don't want to hear another word from Tessa until I have her behind closed doors and up against the wall … and, with that thought, my dick comes to life. *Traitor.*

Reece discusses promoting Don's recent Warwick Award win, that thankfully no one here attended. Then the meeting adjourns, and everyone leaves the room except Reece, Tessa, and me.

Reece stands next to Tessa, talking softly to her and looking my way. She's likely telling Tessa I don't normally act like such a jackass, and it's true. I have a reputation for being tough but fair—not a person who shoots down a new hire on their first damn day. I drag my fingers through my hair, which is probably looking as disastrous as this morning.

"Ms. Young." Reece and Tessa turn my way. One looks at me confused, the other totally dejected. "Could I have a few minutes with Miss Holly to chat with her personally? Call it a post hire interview."

"I think that would be a good idea," Reece says, nodding. "You two need to get to know each other."

I hold back a mocking laugh at Reece's words. Yeah, we know each other pretty damn well. If I close my eyes, I can still hear Tessa's cries as she falls apart underneath me.

"Follow me, Miss Holly," I snap, walking out of the room. My fists are clenched so tight, my knuckles are turning white.

"Yes, sir," she says, and I bite back my anger.

"It's time you told me how you ended up here at Hammond Press," I lead her inside my office, closing the door behind us. "First wearing a trench coat, and now sitting at a boardroom table with me."

36

TESSA

I stand against Barclay's office door. He leans over me, his hands above my head, caging me in. He gazes down at me, our labored breaths filling the silence surrounding us.

"Are you mad at me?" I stare up at him. The warring emotions in his dark eyes send shivers over my skin.

"Livid," he speaks through a clenched jaw, nostrils flaring. I can't bare him being this angry with me.

"I'm sorry." My voice is as unsteady as my legs. Thankfully, the wall holds me up.

"Why didn't you tell me?" he asks, searching my face for an answer.

"I dropped off my résumé last week and didn't hear a thing until this morning. I've messed everything up." I swallow the lump in my throat, trying not to cry. *Will he ever trust me again?*

"HR went over the fraternization rules with you, right?" I nod, biting my lip.

"I texted you right after the job offer, but you must've been too busy," I say in a rush. Barclay leans in closer, his breath against my cheek, and I inhale his clean scent.

"Our being together is strictly forbidden. If there's even a hint that we're sexually involved, I'll be outed and your employment will end. It's the kind of scandal the media pounces on with our names spread across the headlines. Barclay Hammond and his 'young plaything.' This changes everything between us, Tessa."

"I can't call you Barclay anymore, can I?"

"No, but I'd prefer 'sir' over Mr. Hammond."

"Yes, sir."

"That's my sweet girl." He brushes a strand of hair from my cheek.

"And the last time you address me that way."

"Oh God, Tessa. How will I stay away from you now that I've tasted your lips, felt you tremble in my arms? Seeing you here every day is the closest thing to hell a man can imagine."

"I can resign," I suggest without a thought, but it's crazy. *Who quits their dream job the first day?*

"I can't ask that of you, nor you of me," he says.

With the lightest touch, he runs his nose along my jawline and lets his lips linger against my tingling skin. I close my eyes, promising never to forget this moment with him.

I wait for Barclay to kiss me or pull me into his arms, but he doesn't cross that line. Instead, he pulls away from me, stands tall, and stuffs his hands into his pants pockets. An invisible wall is rising between us.

His face changes, hardens, as he reverts to the man who drove away and left me standing alone on the sidewalk. The warmth and tenderness he's shown me is replaced by an impassive mask.

My heart shatters into a million pieces. I may have landed a job beyond my wildest dreams, but I've lost the man of my dreams in the process.

My chin falls to my chest, preparing for the worst, but secretly hoping for a miracle.

"Look at me, Tessa," Barclay demands, sternly. "I can't risk my company. And we've only just begun getting to know each other. You'll find someone." He stops and swallows, revealing a chink in his steel armor. "But it can't be me."

He turns away, moving to stand at the wall of windows behind his desk. His back is to me, and my hands begin to sweat.

He doesn't have to say another word. This is it. We're over.

"Goodbye, Barclay," I whisper, my voice wobbly.

Not waiting for his response, or lack of one, I leave his office and hurry past a startled Mrs. Mackenzie.

"Tessa," his assistant calls out behind me, but I don't answer or stop. I flee to the closest restroom and collapse inside a stall, crying to release the pain inside until I can breathe again.

37

Five days have passed since I last saw Barclay in his office. I overheard he had a sudden business trip overseas, and I welcomed the fact that he wasn't walking around the same office building as me, not to mention the Hammond Hotel— my soon-to-be permanent home.

I dove into my work, spending ten hours a day at my cubicle. The learning curve overwhelmed me, but I tried to focus on one item at a time on my to do list.

My college advisor told me a boss determines how much you love or hate your job, and fortunately, I couldn't have asked for a better one than Ms. Young. She encourages me to be creative and not be afraid of making mistakes.

"What are you doing here?" Ms. Young says, leaning over the wall of my cubicle. She peers down at me, shaking her head. "It's Friday after five. There's a happy hour somewhere in this city with your name on it. Turn off your computer and go. Scoot. Boss's orders."

"Yes, ma'am," I say, giving her a high salute.

"See you Monday morning. And, Miss Holly, great work this week," she adds, and I exhale, feeling my shoulders ease. I want to make a good impression, more than earn my keep, and hopefully she believes I have.

"Thanks for the opportunity and being so helpful."

"We're going to do great things." She gives me a quick nod before leaving.

After saving the document I was working on, I shut down my computer and grab my bag. It's my first weekend in the city as a true New Yorker rather than a wannabe.

I walk the few blocks back to the Hammond with a spring in my step, excited I get to move into my *furnished* apartment tonight. I have so much to be thankful for.

Maggie plans on joining me here later this month. Her mother owns a spa in Monroeville and needs help while one of her massage therapists is on maternity leave. I can't wait until we are living in Manhattan together.

Hammond Press is even covering the cost of shipping my meager belongings to the city. My mother has packed them up for me and arranged the shipment here with Fed Ex. All five boxes will arrive next week.

When I enter the hotel, the manager waves for me to come to the front desk. "Good evening, Miss Holly," he says. "I have something important to share with you."

"Hi, Mr. Presley. What's up?" I wonder if my brother called him to check up on me again. It wouldn't surprise me one bit.

"Mr. Hammond called earlier today." Every muscle in my body stills like I'm sitting on a precipice. "He asked us to bring all your personal items up to the new apartment from your hotel room, along with fully stocking your fridge. Both were completed this afternoon, so you're all set."

"Wow. This is very unexpected. Thank you," I sputter in shock.

I find it hard to believe Barclay did this for me after he said we were over and hasn't made any contact with me all week. I thought he'd cut me off cold turkey. Maybe he's feeling guilty and this is his way to say he's sorry we had to end it. I've never dated anyone seriously and need a roadmap to find my way with him.

"Just doing my job. You should thank Mr. Hammond. It was all his idea," the manager explains with a smile. "Have a great weekend, miss."

"You too."

Should I thank Barclay? It's a no-brainer. My southern manners will nag at me until I do.

With no need to go back to my hotel room, I fish my apartment key out of my bag and ride the elevator up to my new floor. Mrs. Ratner mentioned a young accountant named Mark, who's also a recent hire, lives across the hall from me. She said it would be nice for us to meet, under the circumstances of us both being new to the city. I'm certain she was playing matchmaker.

Exiting the elevator, I notice the hallways are cozier than the modern hotel floor I've been staying on. The walls and carpet have soft, muted colors. There's even a conversational area with couches and tables near the elevators.

I find my door and stand in front of it. My hand shakes with excitement as I turn the key, entering my *own* apartment in New York City!

I flip on the light switch for the main living area, and I'm hit with a vision of pink. Pillows, accent covers, an upholstered ottoman—all in the shade of my favorite color. It looks like Lily Pulitzer moved to Manhattan.

Behind me, I hear someone say my name. "Hi, Tessa. Do you mind if I come in?"

It takes me two seconds to recognize Mrs. Mackenzie's voice. I spin around to see her smiling face. She stopped by my cubicle and congratulated me on the job the day after I left Barclay's office in tears.

"Yes, please." I motion for her to cross the threshold. I forgot to close the door in my hurry to get inside.

"I'm sorry to drop in uninvited, but I wanted to give you an apartment warming gift." She hands me a pink gift bag, the long kind used for bottles of wine.

"Thank you. You really didn't need to do this. Would you like to come in and sit down?" I ask.

"Maybe another time. My husband and I have dinner reservations soon and he doesn't do late." She laughs, clutching her pearl necklace. "Besides, you need to get settled in. It's your first night here, right?"

"It is. I actually just walked through the door for the first time."

"Well, I won't keep you, but I wanted to tell you something first. If you can spare a minute?" she inquires in a serious tone. Her bubbly mood has disappeared.

"Absolutely. Are you sure you don't want to come in?"

"It's best I don't. What I have to tell you concerns Barclay. And you." She pauses, and I know in an instant what she's really referring to. I nod, unable to deny it. "I've never interfered with his personal life, but this time, I must. He's been a *'complete bear,'* those are Don Black's words, since you left his office on Monday. I don't need the specifics between you guys, but wanted to ask if you'd reach out to him. He needs a friend."

"But the rules," I declare.

"The rules don't say you can't be Barclay's friend. It would be better than nothing. Don't you agree?"

I can't decide if she's pushing us into dangerous waters or ones where Barclay and I can stay afloat, never crossing the lines.

"I appreciate you telling me this. I haven't heard a thing from him since Monday, then he left the country."

"The trip wasn't really needed for business. I believe he wanted to escape the feelings he has for you. He landed back here around three this afternoon. Think about what I said, dear. I better go, or my husband will be in a sour mood." She gives me a motherly hug, and I fight back tears.

After she leaves, I open the gift bag and take out a bottle of red wine. I don't even know if I have a corkscrew in the kitchen, but I find one in short order and pour a glass. The wine tastes smooth on my tongue—and expensive. I sip it while I put away the few things I have in my suitcase, which doesn't even fill-up one-fourth of the closet.

I have another glass of wine and sit on my couch, gazing at my phone. The text thread I've had with Barclay is displayed and my finger hovers over the screen. Finally, I decide to reach out to him, starting with a sincere thank you.

Hey. Thx for the help w/ my apartment. I <3 it. PINK

An hour passes without a reply from Barclay. I resort to viewing TV on my laptop, because the one in the apartment didn't come with a dummy manual. I suck at technology.

I watch a couple episodes of *Sex and the City*, and for a good reason. If anyone knows about man trouble, especially in New York City, it's these women. I'm drinking my third glass of wine without any food, so I eat some microwave popcorn: the dinner of lazy couch potatoes.

My phone pings, and I jump, spilling the popcorn all over the floor. At least the wine stayed upright.

My popcorn-greased fingers fumble with the phone. I peer at the preview screen and gasp.

It's Barclay.
Can I call you?
Sure.
Oh my God.

38

TESSA

My phone rings, and Barclay's name lights up the screen. I freak out and stare at it for a beat. Holding my hand to my chest, I accept the call. Before I speak, I hear the unmistakable wail of a baby crying in the background.

"Barclay? Is that you?"

"Oh, Jesus. Tessa. I'm babysitting my niece and can't get her to stop crying." He sounds frantic and distressed. "It's been over an hour."

He tries to quiet the baby with soothing shushes, but she continues to scream. Poor baby. Poor Barclay.

"Have you changed her diaper or tried feeding her?" I ask, listing off the basic baby needs.

"Yes, all of those. And more than once. I'm at my wit's end on how to help her."

"Her cries sound like she's in pain. Maybe it's gas? Have you tried burping her?"

"What do you mean?" he shoots back at me. Bless his heart. He has no clue. No wonder the sweet thing's hurting.

"Babies take in too much air when eating—"

"I need help," he groans. "I'm sending my driver to pick you up."

"Until I get there, place her on your shoulder and lightly tap her back between her shoulder blades."

"Will do," he says, and the line goes dead.

I glance down at my Betty Boop PJ short set. Yeah, I need to change, especially since the no bra, half-my-boobs-hanging-out look isn't appropriate with how things have changed between us.

I jump over the spilled popcorn on the floor and scurry to my closet. After slipping on a pair of jeans and a soft pink camisole, I thread my toes through my favorite flip-flops and race to meet his driver in front of the hotel. The sidewalk spins in my rush. I shouldn't have started that third glass.

Ten minutes later, with instructions from his driver, I'm knocking on his sister's apartment door in the Upper East Side. I press my ear against the door, listening for a baby's cry, but hear nothing. It's a good sign.

Barclay opens the door, and I hardly recognize him. His hair looks like a blender attacked it, a cloth diaper drapes over his shoulder, and his navy polo is covered in baby powder. He gazes at me with a look of surprised terror. He has babysitting PTSD.

"Are you okay?" I ask.

"I am now. She fell asleep." He exhales and drags his hands over his face. "You were right about the burp. I had no idea a baby that small could belch like a frat boy drinking beer."

"Can I come in or do you want me to leave now that everything's okay?" I shift on my feet, hoping he wants me to stay.

"Oh, shit," he says, moving out of the entryway. "Would you mind staying for a while in case she wakes up?"

No woman would tell a smoking hot, six-foot-three man covered in baby powder no. Even if he's her boss's boss.

"Of course. I've been babysitting since I was fourteen."

He lays a hand on my shoulder, leaning into me. "Thank you, Tessa." His touch isn't meant to be sexual in nature, but my nipples harden and a place low within me clenches. He quickly removes his hand. I'm sure my face shows the effect he has on me.

I walk past him into the main living area, needing some space, and glance around in shock. "It looks like a baby tornado hit," I say, laughing.

Diapers are strewn across the floor and couch and bottles sit on every flat surface available, including expensive looking antiques. I count five pacifiers on just the coffee table.

"I thought I could handle a sweet baby for the night, apparently not," he says with a huff.

"Yeah, I'd say the baby showed you who was boss."

I help Barclay clean up the mess, and check in on his niece, Beatrice, who's sleeping like an angel in her crib. She has a mop of curly hair the shade of Barclay's, and her long black eyelashes rest against chubby cheeks. She's adorable. I wish she were awake to play with, but I'll keep that thought to myself.

I tiptoe out of the room, and Barclay's leaning against the wall, looking like he ran a marathon. I bite down on my lower lip, trying so hard not to laugh.

"I know. I know," he says, smiling at me. "I suck at babies."

"You just need some coaching." We stand in the hallway, gazing at each other, awkwardness growing by the second. Maybe it's time for me to go.

"Would you like a drink? God knows I could use one."

I nod, though it feels like there's a large elephant in the room we aren't addressing. Basically, I shouldn't be here alone.

"Maybe a diet soda or something. I've already had two, working on three glasses of red wine tonight, so no more alcohol. Mrs. Mackenzie gave me the bottle." Barclay raises a brow at the mention of his assistant, but doesn't ask anything further. I follow him to a sparkly kitchen with shiny granite counters and stainless steel.

"Have you eaten dinner?"

"Just popcorn."

"Tessa, that's not food. I'm ordering pizza from John's. Have you tried it yet?" He hands me a drink.

"Thanks," I say, lifting the glass. "It's been the dollar slice life for me. The cheap place by the office, and it's not even worth a buck."

"That's like eating cardstock with tomato sauce. John's it is." Barclay pulls out his phone to call in the order, and a pacifier tumbles out of his pocket, landing on floor. We both stare at it and laugh until we're in tears.

"Hey," Barclay says, after calling in the pizza order. "Let's play a little game while we wait."

"What do you have in mind?" I ask, giving him a pointed stare.

"We'll ask each other a few what or why questions. For instance, why do you always wear pink?"

"So, you're going to start with that one?" I ask, and he laughs.

"Yeah, I guess I am." We take a seat on the couch with a comfortable friend-zone distance between us.

"After having a boy, my mother loved dressing me in pink frilly clothes. One day, I asked her why the boys at preschool didn't wear pink, but the girls could wear blue. She told me it was because pink gave me a special superpower and I believed her. So every day, I have to wear something with pink in it."

"I do believe she's right," Barclay says, his eyes darkening. "The color looks lovely on you, Tessa.

"Thank you," I say, blushing pink, of course. "Okay, my turn. Are there any rules?"

I give him the once over, contemplating how far I want to stick the knife.

"Nope," he quips, and I take a deep breath.

"Okay, then. Why isn't there a Mrs. Hammond, or a soon to be one?" I go for the throat. After all, he's thirty-seven. In Alabama, guys that age have kids in middle school.

"Honest?" he asks, and I nod, watching him squirm. "Well, I've never been with anyone who made me want this." He gestures around the room full of baby gear and wedding photos. All scream one thing: commitment.

Considering how I feel so drawn to him, maybe not being together isn't such a bad thing in the end. He's the kind of man who could tear my heart to shreds.

An hour later, we're sitting on the couch eating pizza. Neither of us has mentioned anything related to me working at Hammond, or us being together last Saturday night. But with the dinner over, I can feel the unspoken words hanging in the air.

Which one of us will be brave enough to broach the subject?

"Tessa." He turns toward me on the couch, but the way he said my name makes the atmosphere shift from casual fun to serious. "I want to talk to you about Monday. I should've handled the whole thing better. I did some digging around and confirmed what you told me."

"It's okay. I have to take the blame for not telling you I

dropped off my résumé and about my blog, especially after Don mentioned it."

"But the thing is, even after a week away from you, you're all I think about. Day and night. When I get my coffee, I remember the day I met you. I even had a cherry tart while in Paris. And I'm not a big fan."

"Me too. Well not the coffee or cherry tart in Paris. More just sleeping in my bed alone. It's then that I think about you the most ..." my voice trails off, and his eyes darken.

"Do you miss me?" he asks in almost a whisper, daring to brush a hair off my cheek, leaving a tingle over my skin.

"Yes, so much it hurts." My voice cracks as I speak through the pain in my chest.

"I feel like I'll go mad if I don't have you in my arms again," he says, an aching longing in his voice.

"This isn't helping Barclay." I glance away, because looking at this beautiful man with troubled eyes breaks me.

"Text me when you get lonely and miss me. There's nothing wrong with us doing that."

I nod, looking up at him with cloudy eyes. Why does he have to be so perfect?

"Ah, fuck, don't cry, Tessa. I want to be with you too. For now, sweet girl, all we can do is be friends. I miss you too much to have you completely out of my life."

He reaches for my hand, encircling it with his. His thumb brushes my knuckles in a rhythmic back and forth motion, and my breaths become deeper, quicker. It's simply too much, but I can't move away from him. I need this connection.

We stay locked in this position for minutes, gazing at each other with faraway eyes, imagining dreams that can't be realized.

"I can live with that. For now," I whisper.

39

Two weeks have passed since the babysitting fiasco night, or as I call it, the beginning of our platonic relationship, and it was the last time I've been alone with Tessa. We've shared crowded elevators at work. Sent friendly texts. I made sure mine were all innocent in nature, because the dirty things I want to tell her would get me fired and her dismissed.

Our hungry glances across the boardroom table during the weekly marketing meetings have left me aching to touch her soft skin again, kiss her lips, and devour every inch of her. Occasionally, I'm close enough to catch her perfume in the air. Even now, if I close my eyes, I can imagine her scent. It's sealed in my memory as a form of self-torture.

Being apart from her hasn't separated me from her. I feel an invisible thread connecting us, making me hyperaware of her presence. That's how I know she arrived, at my father's birthday party, before I even see her. I feel her essence in the air like a mist cooling my skin.

"Barc," my sister says, grabbing my attention. We're leaning against the terrace balustrade connected to my parents' home. The party is below us on the lawn. "Isn't that Tessa, the young woman you brought to the Warwick Awards? Over there by the pool house, next to the bar."

I find Tessa before my sister finishes her question. She's wearing the same dress from the night we first saw each other. Her shoulders are creamy smooth, and showcased by pink ruffles. I swallow back my desire for her with a swig of my bourbon.

"Yes, that's her." My voice is impassive, giving nothing away, while knowing my inquisitive sister will work me until she knows everything.

"Is she here as your date?" She turns toward me, scanning my face for a crack in my armor, and she'll find it if she looks close enough.

"No," I quip, watching Tessa beam at Mark, the new hire in accounting. "She works at Hammond now."

My jaw tenses when he places his hand on the small of her back and leads her to the banquet buffet. As they walk together, he catches a lock of her hair and releases it. My fingers tighten around my bourbon glass. I'm surprised it doesn't shatter to pieces. The fucker wants her.

"Goodness, Barc," Victoria says with a pained tone. "You've fallen in love with her, haven't you?"

I turn to face my sister, letting her witness my agony. She places a hand on my arm, tilting her head and sighing, knowing my answer without me uttering a word.

"Does Mother know?" Her eyes fill with concern.

"No one knows, and it has to stay that way. She's my employee. We can never happen."

"I'm sorry, Barc. I wish there was something I could do."

I linger on the terrace long after Victoria leaves, only joining the party after I've finished off my drink and need a refill.

Another bourbon later, I'm mingling with the crowd of revelers. It will likely be my father's last executive birthday party. The doctors say his memory for faces and names may not last another year. But today, he seems on top of the world as everyone wishes him happy birthday.

Not far from my father, I watch Tessa and Mark. He says something to her, and she hesitates, looking away. When she glances back at him, her lips form the word, *"okay."* Mark answers with a smile saved for winning a million-dollar lottery, because I believe he won something more worthy than he deserves. *Her.*

I stride toward them, needing to know if she's agreed to go out with him. My stomach twists at the thought of this man's hands on her. As I near them, I slow my pace and take a couple breaths, trying to regain control of this fire racing through my veins.

"Hello, Barc—I mean, Mr. Hammond," Tessa says. Her bright blue eyes dart between Mark and me in worry.

"Mr. Hammond," Mark addresses me. I stuff my hands inside my pockets before he tries to shake either one. *Very grown up, Barclay.* "Great party, sir."

"Yes, some of us seem to be enjoying it more than others," I scoff, causing Mark to look at me confused.

"I think he means some people have nothing left in their glass." Tessa holds up an empty champagne flute for the save. Southern women and their polished manners.

"Here, let me get you another. I'll be right back." Mark takes her glass and scurries toward the bar like a love-struck man. *Bastard.*

"Barc," Tessa warns through a fake smile. "What's the matter with you? All the executive staff is here, so you better be careful."

"What did he ask you?" I demand.

"Oh God, please not here." She lowers her head, shaking it.

"Follow me and plaster on a big fat grin like you mean it."

I casually lead her across the manicured grass to the stone patio. Since everyone's mixing company ranks at the party, no one seems to take notice of us.

Our final destination is a game room inside the lower level. I open the patio French doors for Tessa and glance back toward the party. I can't see anyone, even at my height, meaning we're hidden from prying eyes.

"Through the doors and to the right. The room with the

pool table," I tell her, and Tessa follows my orders, but her searching eyes show concern.

Once we're both in the room, I close the door and lock it. There aren't any outside windows, so we have total privacy. Tessa leans her lovely ass against the pool table, arms across her chest. I stalk toward her, placing my hands on either side of her thighs, gripping the felt covered edge of the table.

I stare down at her. She has eyes like the clearest morning sky, pouty lips begging for my kisses, and a hint of cleavage that drives me insane.

"What's going on with *Mark*?" I say his name with disgust. Tessa avoids my question and glances down at the floor.

"Please answer me?" I ask quieter, ratcheting down my anger laced voice. "I shouldn't take out my frustrations on you."

"You don't think I'm frustrated too?" She meets my gaze, fire in her eyes. "Being so near you at the office. Friendly texts with you when I'd rather be doing other things. It's driving me mad."

She pushes one of my hands off the pool table, freeing herself, then walks away from me. When she stops, I notice her slumped shoulders slightly moving up and down. *Shit,* I've made her cry.

Unable to keep a proper distance from her, I turn her toward me and pull her into my arms. She folds into my chest, so small and delicate. I want to tell her it's going to be okay, wash away her hurt, but I don't see a way out of our dilemma. She begins to calm as I caress her back in soothing motions.

"Just being friends isn't working out very well, is it, sweet girl?" She peers up at me with soft, watery eyes that break my heart. A tear falls down her cheek, and I brush it away.

"It's horrible, Barclay." Her voice quivers. "I met your father today. He's a lovely man, just like you. The consequence of us being together became more real to me. I only have a lifestyle to lose, find another job in the city or elsewhere, but your loss is a legacy built by your father. I can't be the woman who causes it to burn to the ground."

"What are you trying to say?" I ask.

"I think it's best if we quit texting each other and take a break. It's just too hard being this close to you while wanting more."

"So, you're going to go out with him then."

"Just to a Yankee's game tomorrow as friends."

"No man, including me, can ever be just friends with you. Haven't the last few weeks proven that?" I place a finger under her chin, lifting it higher. "Can I do one thing before you walk out of my life for good?"

"What is it?" she breathes.

"May I kiss you?"

She closes her eyes and exhales, and my pulse races as I wait.

"Yes," she whispers, opening her eyes.

Our lips touch, moving slowly and sweetly at first. Tentative. But as we continue, the passion we've suppressed turns into a raging blaze of need and desire. She places her hands beneath my shirt, touching me with a simple graze of her fingers. The initial feelings are too much, and I flinch as if burned. But nothing holds her back—or me.

I kiss over the curve of her throat, continuing to the swell of her breasts. Wanting more access, I push her over-the-shoulder dress down, exposing a lacy strapless bra. It's virginal white, and I lose my mind. I reach into each cup, freeing her breasts, and take them into my mouth one by one. When my tongue flicks her nipple, she moans and weaves her hands through my hair, pulling the strands.

I back her up against the nearest wall, wrapping her legs around my waist. Her hot center meets my hard cock. The feel of her is torturous ecstasy. I take her hands in mine and raise them over her head, pinning her to the wall. Our gazes lock in that moment like a slap to the face.

"Barclay?" she asks, her voice cracking.

"I know, Tessa. I know." I bury my face in the crook of her neck and breath her in. If I can't consume her with my body, at least I can store away her scent.

After a minute, I release her hands and adjust her bra and dress, fixing the results of my out of control passion. When I step away from the wall, I lower her legs to the ground, and a distant chill cools the fire in my veins.

"I better go," she says, eyes looking at anything but me.

After smoothing her blond hair and straightening her dress, she's gone, likely heading back to the party and starry-eyed Mark. I slump against the pool table, arms spread wide on the edge and head hanging low.

I hear someone enter the room and immediately hope it's her returning to me.

"Tessa?" I call out as I turn around, but it's my mother standing just inside the door. She's looking at me with sadness etched across her face. It's an expression I've seen countless times over the years, especially when I'm hurting and need her help or comfort. This time, neither is possible.

"Oh, Barclay," she says, walking toward me, taking me in her arms. "Tessa's the young woman your sister told me about."

She releases me from her arms and pulls back to look up into my eyes. It's strange how blurry she appears at this moment.

"Yes, she's the one." There's no use hiding anything from her. A mother always knows.

"Believe it or not, I understand all too well what you're going through. As you know, your father and I fell madly in love when I came to work for him, but it was a different time in the corporate world. Today, the rules are less forgiving."

"I fell for her before she was hired. Hell, I was the last one to know she had gotten the job, but the no-fraternization rules are clear. We can't be together, and I'm the company's leader. One mess up from me and everyone pays."

"I have an idea." I see the wheels turning in her smiling blue eyes. "Don't give up just yet, son."

40

TESSA

"I had a great time at the game tonight. Thanks," I tell Mark. We're standing together outside my apartment door. "I should've split the cost of the tickets with you, though."

The fact that he lives across the hall makes this goodbye awkward. Actually, it makes all things awkward, because I only see him as a friend.

"It was my pleasure, really," he says, looking from my eyes to my lips.

Oh no! Is he going to kiss me? Barclay was right about one thing: he likes me in the more-than-a-friend way. I've been picking up those vibes from him all night.

I pull my bag open and start digging around for my keys. Anything to distract him from kissing me.

"Here they are." I hold my keys up in the air, conveniently filling the space between us and hoping he takes the hint.

But he doesn't. He springs forward, his arm landing on my shoulder as his mouth connects with mine in a wet, sloppy kiss, reminiscent of licks from a happy puppy. I pull away and wipe my lips.

Gross.

He turns scarlet, as he should. "How dare you kiss me like that?"

"I'm sorry," he says with sad eyes and a deflated stance.

Truly sorry or not, he needs to know exactly how I feel about him. At this point, he gives me the damn creeps.

"That kiss was presumptive, Mark." I place a hand on my hip, and he retreats a step. "It's not like we're five years old on the playground. Your approach was way too aggressive for me."

"Are you going to tell Mr. Hammond?"

"Barclay?" I ask. He tilts his head, then his eyes narrow, assessing me.

I cover my mouth in shock, realizing I used his first name —something a junior executive doesn't do at Hammond.

"I saw you two going toward the house, alone. Then you were upset when you came back to the party." Mark searches my face, looking for a slip, but I won't give him one.

"I was looking for the restroom and Mr. Hammond showed

me the one inside," I lie without any regrets, because I won't let him expose the man I ... *I love?* It's the first time I've admitted it to myself, but I love him madly, more than a dream job.

What good will it be if I don't have him? The question gives me an epiphany, and I have to act on it now.

"I have to go, Mark." I spin around and unlock my door.

After booting up my laptop, I open my company email program and start an email to Ms. Young.

Dear Ms. Young,

I want to thank you for the opportunity you gave me at Hammond Press and the confidence you have in my abilities. For reasons I can't discuss, unfortunately, I must resign as junior marketing manager effective immediately.

Sincerely,

Contessa Holly

My finger hovers over the mouse, knowing one click changes my world ... for today. The chances are I'll land another publishing gig or something close, but will I find another man like Barclay—one I love with my whole heart, and who I think loves me?

I press send. He's worth the gamble. I refuse to live my life with what ifs. My new motto: live my life with no regrets. And my new goal, for tonight anyway: find Barclay and lose *it*.

I change out of the clothes I wore to the baseball game with creepy Mark and shower off any remnants of his DNA. I brush my hair and reapply my makeup. Next up, what to wear.

Maggie bought me a sexy pink slip dress before I left town. It's street wear lingerie and perfect for tonight. I leave my undergarments sitting in the dresser drawer all alone, and make my way up to the top floor of Hammond Hotel.

I step off the elevator, and bottled up emotions come bubbling up. I just quit my job and can finally be his. Nothing stands in our way. Shaky legs carry me to the hallway and the lone apartment door on the entire floor. I inhale confidence and exhale fear before I push the doorbell, praying he's home.

A beat later, the door opens, and a disheveled Barclay stands in the doorway. His hair's mussed in every direction and a delicious layer of scruff covers his chiseled jaw. He's wearing an unbuttoned white linen shirt, displaying cut abs, and jeans that hang low enough that I can see the edge of his boxer briefs.

"How was your date, sweet girl?" he snarls at me, a slight slur to his words. The smell of strong alcohol on his breath lingers in the air.

He's *drunk*, with a fiery passion in his eyes that could ruin me if it's let loose, and I've never wanted anything so much.

41

BARCLAY

I lean my hand against the doorframe, steadying myself after spending the evening with a bottle of bourbon. It was a wasted effort in the end, because nothing is powerful enough to erase Tessa from my mind … and heart.

She taunts me, standing in the hallway looking so fucking beautiful in a barely-there dress revealing dangerous curves my fingers itch to touch again. Her hard nipples are outlined in perfect detail, as if she's bare underneath. I can only take so much before I cross the line I'm trying to balance on.

"You were right," she whispers, gazing up at me. "Mark wanted more."

"Did he try to kiss or touch you?" My angry voice fills the air between us. How dare he take what should be mine?

"When he tried to kiss me, it was horrible, Barclay." Her voice cracks as she walks toward me, eyes shining with unshed tears. "He wasn't you, and I wanted him to be you so bad."

Between Tessa's pleas and my bourbon-soaked brain, the last bit of my resolve melts away. I know one thing: I never want to spend another night without her again.

"Rules be damned. Tonight, you're going to be mine," I growl, taking hold of her hand and drawing her inside my apartment. With a quick kick, I close the door and the world behind us.

She tries to speak, but I claim her mouth, silencing her with a long kiss. I inch my fingers under her dress to grab her ass and find her bare underneath.

"Are you trying to kill me? Running around without anything under this flimsy material. Tell me you didn't go out with him like this."

"It's just for you," she breathes. "I need to tell you something, Barclay."

"You're telling me all I need to hear with your lips on mine," I whisper, showering her neck with kisses. "We can talk later."

"Mmhmm," she mutters, melting into my arms. Finally.

"I'm taking you to my bed," I announce, scooping her up in my arms, her hands encircling my neck.

"Yes, please." She gives me a shy, sweet smile, reminding me of her innocence and how special this night is for her.

Entering my master suite, I hold her closer, needing to calm any fears she may have. "I'll do everything to make it good for you. Will you trust me, Tessa?"

She peeks up at me through her lashes, eyes bright. "I'm all yours. I want you to be the one." She brings her lips to mine in a scorching kiss.

42

He handles me like I'm made of fragile glass and eases me down on the large master bed. It fits the room and the man. The lights are turned off, but the city glows through a wall of windows, sending moving shadows across the ceiling and walls.

He stands a few feet away from the bed and removes his shirt. The lighting is muted, but I can still make out his carved abs. I wish he wasn't beyond my reach. I want to touch him so bad.

Piece by piece, he undresses himself until there's only one more item of clothing left: his boxer briefs. I wait for the reveal, and when he pushes them down his legs, I gasp. He's long and hard—gravity defying. *My word.* Seeing a naked man on the internet is nothing compared to the vision of Barclay in person. I can't quit staring at his perfection.

The dark shadows mix with the dim light and crisscross over his body, making him look like a granite statue of masculine beauty. I glance up at his face to find him smirking at me, knowing I've been caught ogling him.

"Raise your hands over your head, baby." I do as he asks, and he removes my dress, stepping back to ogle me. "You're lovely beyond words."

I fight the urge to cover myself as his eyes pore over every inch of my exposed skin. Barclay must sense my unease, and brushes my cheek in a lingering touch. It's so tender and caring, all my self-conscious feelings begin to fade away.

"No man can ever be fully worthy of you, Tessa, but I'll try." My eyes cloud with tears knowing how he sees me, even if I don't believe it myself.

"I want you, Barclay. Only you."

He reaches into his nightstand, pulls out a foiled square and a bottle filled with a clear lubricant, and places them on the bed.

"I've wanted you since the first time I saw you sitting in the restaurant, so pretty in pink, coloring the space around you. With your blond hair caressing shoulders I longed to touch. I couldn't get you off my mind."

His hands gently spread my legs apart, then he positions

himself over me. He kisses my lips, then takes my nipple into his mouth and does that trick with his tongue that drives me wild. I grab hold of his hair for dear life.

"You really like that." He chuckles.

"Please, don't stop," I beg.

"Never," he exclaims, moving lower and trailing his lips over my stomach, stopping at the valley where my hips and thighs meet. When he sucks the tender skin there, I arch my back off the bed and whimper.

His tongue and fingers find my aching center and join to work me into a moaning frenzy.

"Barclay," I moan. "I had no idea."

"This is only the beginning, sweet girl. There are so many things I want to do to you."

Somewhere in the lust-filled haze of his touches, I hear him tear the foil pack. He kneels between my legs, coating the condom with lubricant.

I stare at the beauty of him in complete awe. Powerful thighs, a cut jawline set hard while he concentrates on his task. This moment is more than I'd ever dreamed of for my first time, and my heart flutters in anticipation as our eyes lock. This is it, *finally*.

"Are you sure, Tessa?" he asks, anxious eyes waiting for my reply.

"Yes, please. There's no one I'd rather be with than you." He smiles down at me with a heady mix of lust and adoration.

Positioning himself at my entrance, he gently pushes

inside me, and by some miracle, I begin to stretch with him. He stares intently at me, watching for my every reaction and feeling.

When he reaches a point of resistance, he thrusts against it, and I feel a flash of pain that steals my breath.

Our eyes meet at the exact moment he's fully seated inside of me, and we both know I'm no longer a virgin. Instead, I'm fully and completely his.

"Are you okay, sweet girl?" he whispers, in a gentle voice. "I want this to be so good for you. It's all that matters to me."

"Yes," I say. "It's perfect because I'm with you."

After a beat, he moves inside me, until the pinch begins to subside. I wrap my legs around his waist, raising my hips to meet his movements, wanting him to know I'm all right.

"Tell me I'll be your last," he breathes, possessing me with the deepest kiss.

"The only one," I sigh against his lips.

The pain turns to pleasure as he makes love to me in a sweet and gentle rhythm. Then he teases my most sensitive spot with his finger, making slow circles, and I know my release is seconds away.

"Come for me, sweet girl," he says, coaxing with his words and touch.

My orgasm rushes over me, and I'm lost to the feelings as he continues his movements inside me.

When I open my eyes and gaze up at this beautiful man who holds my heart, his eyes reflect a wild desperation as he falls over the edge too.

"Tessa," he hisses in a long breath.

The look on his face, the pained pleasure etched in the strain of his jaw, will forever be burned in my memory.

After we both catch our breaths, he rests his forehead against mine with a sigh. His breath smells of bourbon and spice like a man, and I inhale deeper.

"Thank you, sweet girl," he says. "You okay?"

"Amazing," I say with the most contented smile.

He gives me a quick kiss before getting up to discard the condom. I bite my lip as he strides away to the en suite bath, watching the slightest jiggle in his tight butt. I fall back on the bed in a swoon.

When he returns, he puts his underwear back on, and walks toward the bed. I think he's going to climb in beside me, but he wraps the white bedspread around me like a cocoon and cradles me in his arms instead.

"I want to show you something," he says, carrying me toward a set of French doors.

"Open it, please." He bends down, and I turn the knob, pushing the door free from the inside. He pads outside onto a large terrace filled with loungers and table sets.

He eases us down on one of the loungers, and I lie back against his chest. "Look up," he says, and I do. "There's nothing between us and the universe in the night's summer sky."

"It's beautiful," I say, gazing up at the twinkling stars shining brighter than the city lights.

"But not as beautiful as you," he marvels.

He folds me tighter into his arms and we stare at the sky, listening to the humming white noise of the city below. And somewhere in the warmth of his embrace, I drift off, lulled to sleep by the rise and fall of his chest.

43

TESSA

"Tessa," Barclay calls, pulling my brain out of its slumber. "Time to wake up, sleepy head."

"Go away," I mutter, refusing to open my eyes. He's interrupting a beautiful dream of last night with him. "My dream was just getting to the good part."

"And what part might that be?" he asks, stroking my cheek.

The man isn't letting up on getting me up, so I give in and peek at him through fluttering lashes. My eyes go wide at the sight before me. He's sitting on the edge of the bed decked out in an onyx colored suit that matches the color of his smoky eyes. His wavy black hair is perfectly smoothed back, and he smells divine. I want to grab him by his red silk tie and drag him back to bed with me.

"You're too handsome and tempting for this early in the morning."

Since I fell asleep without clothes on, I pull the soft sheets up to my neck and move to sit beside him. Unable to fight his magnetic presence, I run a finger along his lapel, toying with one of the buttons on his jacket.

"It's not that early, sweetheart," he says, pointing to the clock on the nightstand. Eight thirty. Whoa, he's right.

If I were still employed at Hammond Press, I'd have to be at my desk, computer fired up, and ready to roll in thirty minutes, which makes me wonder why Barclay didn't wake up sooner. Just like I feared, I'm already getting preferential treatment by being in his bed.

"Last night ... I should've told you something before we did all this." I glance away from his intense gaze and take a deep breath for courage.

In the light of day, and without all the raging hormones blurring my thoughts, I regret not telling him about the resignation letter before I took one step inside his door. In my defense, I was helpless when he silenced me with searing kisses and a talented tongue, but still, I wasn't honest with him.

"Hush." He quiets me, placing a long finger over my lips. "I know all about your email to Reece."

"You do?" My mouth drops open, and his lips tilt up in the hottest, I-know-it-all smirk.

"Reece emailed while I was drinking my coffee. It woke me up better than the caffeine." He regards me in an impassive manner. It's a powerplay expression that works in the boardroom, but not so much in the bedroom.

"Are you upset with me?" I ask.

"Well, Reece isn't accepting your resignation via email, and as your boss's boss, neither am I. We want you in the office by ten." He adjusts his shiny cufflinks and stands, dismissing further conversation on the matter.

"I'm leaving Hammond. And there's nothing that will change my mind." I stand up next to him in a huff, attempting to drape the long sheet around me, but end up looking like a half-nude mummy.

"This is a bit of overkill." The sexy devil laughs at my expense, tugging at the sheet. "Since I've already seen and kissed every inch of you."

"I'm aware of this fact." I sigh, my eyes going all dreamy, remembering his lips on me everywhere.

"And we'll see about you leaving. Now, go get ready." When he passes by me, he slaps my ass, though I barely feel it under the wrapped sheets.

"What was that?" I ask in protest, though I actually loved it and hope he does it again.

"Just trying to keep you in line, sweet girl." He walks out the bedroom door and I follow, hot on his trail. "My driver will pick you up promptly at nine forty-five."

"That's not necessary. It's only a few blocks away."

Midtown traffic moves at a snail's pace. I can walk to the building faster—even in heels.

Entering the smooth marble entryway, Barclay stops on a dime, turning around to face me. Unprepared, I slam straight into his hard chest. He grabs hold of my arms and gazes down at me, a mischievous spark in his eyes.

"I want to make sure you're there at ten, so you're being supervised."

"I'm not a child." I cross my arms over my chest, thus pushing my boobs up and nearly over the sheet wrap. Barclay's eyes focus on my prominent cleavage, and he licks his lips.

"Oh, believe me, Tessa. I'm quite aware you're a woman." He takes me in his arms and gives me a scorching kiss, leaving me breathless. "See you soon, beautiful."

I stare at the closed door long after he's gone, wondering what's so important about me coming in today. Shouldn't an email suffice? Maybe it's just a formality, but my southern intuition tells me the suited sex god is up to something. Perhaps we've both been less than forthcoming.

"Good morning, Miss Holly," Lawrence says as I climb into the back of the car. "You're looking lovely today."

"Thank you." His compliment seems genuine, and I appreciate it. I want to make a good impression when I walk into Hammond on my last official day.

When we arrive at the building, I exit the car and hold my head high as I walk inside the lobby where it all began with spilled coffee.

I take the elevator to the top floor and plant myself in my chair at precisely ten. My cubicle is exactly as I left it on Friday—sticky notes scattered along the sidewall and artwork for the Hamming It Up Instagram campaign lying next to my computer.

I can't deny I feel horribly sad and disappointed knowing this will be my last time sitting here. I only just began chasing my dream, and I loved everything about the job, except it's dating policy.

Grabbing a tissue from the box on my desk, I dab my eyes. I know I made the right decision to leave in the end, but facing what I'll miss head-on makes my heart hurt. I wish they accepted my email resignation instead of subjecting me to this torture.

I sit at my desk and make a list of other companies that were once interested in me. I canceled their interviews after I accepted my position and sold my blog to Hammond Press. Poor Shakespurr is out of my hands now, and that stings the worst.

"Good morning, Tessa." Ms. Young, my soon to be ex-boss, startles me from my thoughts. She leans over my cubicle with an odd smile on her face. At least she's not mad at me, or is faking it, but that's not her style.

"Good morning?" I say, confused all around with the way she's treating me under the circumstances.

"Mr. Hammond will see you now," she laughs, confounding me even more. I see no humor in this entire matter. "Along with his mother."

"Huh?" I say my thoughts out loud. *What does his mother have to do with me quitting?*

"I was right about the two of you," she says, nodding with that same strange smile spread across her face. "I'd watch him staring at you with this sad, longing look during our marketing meetings. Hell, the sexual tension was hot enough to melt the paint off the walls. Besides, I'm good at spotting a man in love."

"In love?" I squint my eyes, unsure I heard her correctly.

She bursts out laughing. "You have no idea. Now, get to his office and come back to see me when the meeting's over."

I rise up on shaky legs and make my way down the hallway to Barclay's office suite. It takes all my strength to turn the doorknob and walk inside.

44

"Miss Holly," Mrs. Mackenzie exclaims as she rises from her desk, crossing the room to meet me. "Mr. Hammond and his mother, Sandra, are waiting for you. Follow me, dear."

She gives my arm a reassuring squeeze, along with a tender smile. I imagine I look like I'm headed toward the firing squad.

Mrs. Mackenzie opens Barclay's door, and my feet feel like lead. "It's going to be okay." Mrs. Mackenzie gives me a gentle nod, and I enter.

He's discarded his suit jacket and leans against the edge of his desk. His long legs are crossed at the ankle, appearing casual and relaxed—and hot as hell.

His mother sits demurely in a leather chair to the side of Barclay's desk. It's no guess where Barclay got his glossy black hair. When she smiles at me, her eyes shine as bright as a blue sky. She's wearing a pink suit—Chanel, most likely, from the make and cut. It's my dream work attire.

"Tessa," Barclay says. "This is my mother, Sandra Hammond."

"It's so lovely to meet you, Tessa," she says in a cheery tone, which surprises me. Her son and I have "broken the rules of personal engagement" at Hammond.

"Nice to meet you, ma'am," I reply, making sure to use my southern manners. There's no handshaking or formalities between us either. Everything feels personal.

"I'm sorry we didn't meet at the picnic. I was so busy keeping everything afloat. If we would have run out of food or alcohol, the natives would have worried the company was going under."

We all laugh at her humor. I immediately like her.

"It was a great party," I say. And it's true, even if it ended with Barclay and me fighting about Mark.

"My husband told me he met a lovely young woman from Alabama. Minus the blond hair, he said you reminded him of me. And now, just like his father, Barclay finds himself falling for a southerner who works for him. Funny, isn't it?"

Perhaps it is, but I'm not laughing. I glance at Barclay, worried she knows about us.

"I told my mother our story at the picnic and she started cooking up a workaround for us." He winks at me, and I exhale a deep breath, having a glimmer of hope for the first time.

"Have a seat, and I'll explain," Mrs. Hammond says to me, pointing to the chair across from her. I do as she asks.

"I called for an emergency board meeting this morning," his mother begins. "We've promoted Reece Young to chief marketing officer. It was long overdue. She'll report to board member, Mary Murphy, who was formerly head of marketing for Time Warner. Ms. Young will no longer be in Barclay's chain of command, and most importantly, neither will you."

"We're in the clear," Barclay pushes off the edge of the desk and strides to me. Taking my hand, he pulls me to my feet and gazes down at me with eyes full of hope ... for us.

"I can't believe this," I say, glancing between Barclay and his mother, hardly able to contain myself. "How will I ever be able to thank you?"

"Join our family at the Hamptons this weekend. We want to get to know you better," she says. I look at Barclay, and he nods.

"I'd love too. Thanks," I say in a rush, the excitement bubbling up inside me. I have my dream job—and my dream man. How did this even happen? I'm simply amazed.

"I'd do anything for my son and the woman he wants." She rises out of the chair and straightens her skirt. "I'll leave you two lovebirds alone to celebrate."

As soon as the door closes behind her, Barclay envelops me in his arms, holding me so close, I can barely breathe. His lips skate over my neck, and I lean my head to the side, letting him have better access.

"How do you feel about fettuccine?" Barclay whispers in my ear.

"I love it," I breathe as his hands slip under my skirt, approaching the danger zone.

"Great. There's this little place in Philly that serves the best. I'm having it flown in tonight."

"But there's an Italian restaurant on every block here."

"I only want the best for you." He gazes down at me with heat in his eyes.

"Why are you spoiling me like this?" I ask, secretly loving how he treats me like a queen.

"It's a long list."

"Care to share?" I ask, curious to hear what he thinks about me.

"I'm in love with your smile and sweet innocence." His lips skim my jawline, sending tingles over my skin.

"The way you twirl your hair when you're nervous." He nips at my earlobe, making me squirm in his arms.

"And the dark side of me craves your sinful body." His fingers delve under the lace of my panties, finding the spot yearning for his touch.

"I'm in love with you, Tessa. All of you."

He starts kissing over my cheeks, shushing me, and it's then I realize his lips are wiping away my tears.

"I love you too," I whisper, barely able to speak.

Fate doesn't hate us after all.

45

I pace the sidewalk outside the Hammond Hotel, waiting for Miles and Maggie to arrive with all my earthly possessions from Alabama. Glancing down the one-way street, a U-Haul van comes into view with Maggie waving at me. She beams with excitement as she bounces in the passenger seat.

Before Miles brings it to a complete stop, she jumps out of the van. My brother scowls at her and shakes his head. I have a feeling it's been a long trip for him.

"Oh my God!" she screams, running toward me, her long brown hair flying behind her. "I made it."

"I'm so happy you're finally here." She gives me a big hug

as Miles walks up behind her. His frown has transformed into a broad smile, his eyes sparkling at me.

"Where's my hug? I'm the one who had to put up with her for eleven hundred miles." He embraces me, and it feels so good to be surrounded by his familiar, protective arms. I've missed him so much.

"I'm so glad you're here," I say as he inspects me from head to toe.

"You look happy and have this glow." He tilts his head and rubs his chin. "The city suits you, though part of me hates to admit it. I'd prefer to have you back home."

"Well, there's no place like home, but Manhattan's feeling like my second one," I tell him, and he rolls his eyes, but still with a smile.

"You've done good, little sis."

Miles helps Maggie and I unload our few boxes onto carts provided by the hotel ... or Barclay, really. He made sure we had plenty of help to get what few things I own—all five large boxes—upstairs into my apartment.

My mother packed everything up for me, but I left all my childhood trinkets and memories back in Alabama. For some reason, I wanted to be able to go home and stay in my old room, still surrounded by them. Keep the memories in one place. Maybe later, I'll bring some back, but I want New York City to make its own mark on me for now.

Maggie, Miles, and I are in front of the apartment door with the first load of boxes. I dig the keys out of my pocket.

"Hurry up," Maggie says, but I hand her a set of keys instead of opening the door myself.

"Here are yours." I place a brand new sterling silver Tiffany key chain in the palm of her hand. It was a splurge after my first paycheck.

"*Tessa*. Thank you. " Her eyes cloud as she smiles at me in the sweetest way. It means everything, because we made it. Our dream of living here came true.

My brother leaves Maggie and me alone while we unpack. He wouldn't say what he was up to, but I imagine he's likely grilling the hotel staff about Barclay. Even out of uniform, my brother wears an invisible badge.

I told my family about Barclay and I being together as a couple the day after the company shifted my boss's reporting line. I wanted them to find out from me, not the press or one of the small town's gossips. And believe me, everyone knows everyone's business in Monroeville.

I'd love to say they're all overjoyed I'm dating a thirty-seven-year-old publishing mogul, but that's not totally the case. My mother wants to be understanding and sympathetic. After all, Barclay's from the world of books—her first love. My father feels it's too soon for me to be so serious, and wants me to date around. But I remember what Barclay said about guys in their twenties—they're nothing like the boys in Alabama.

And finally, there's Miles. He's got Barclay pegged as Hollywood's version of a rich Manhattan playboy. Hanging out at all the elite parties. Screwing a different supermodel every night. The list goes on. So to squash his prejudices of the man I love, Miles is meeting Barclay downstairs at the hotel restaurant for drinks and dinner.

The funny thing about this meeting? Miles doesn't have a clue Barclay's been invited. He thinks he's having dinner with Maggie and me. *I can't wait.* The element of surprise will give Barclay the advantage, and that's everything when you're dealing with the world's most overprotective brother and seasoned policeman.

I put the last piece of clothing from the boxes into a drawer and Maggie comes into my room.

"How is this our apartment?" She spins around in glee. "I figured we'd be using milk crates for coffee tables and using blow-up beds for the first year."

"I know." I shut the dresser drawer and we step out of my bedroom. "I walk in every night after work and feel like I've broken into someone else's place. It does seem more real having you here, though."

"Now I just need to find a job. I thought I'd try a spa if I don't land one in accounting right away. At least I'm a licensed masseuse."

"Good idea. I'd try one down on Wall Street. Maybe you'll have a client who can network for you. Or we can ask Barclay about some references."

"Good idea, and thanks about Barclay, but I want to get this job on my own. I want to sit on top of the Empire State Building in victory."

"Exactly how I felt," I say, because she knows the story. I

got my job at Hammond Press on my own, even if Trevor did help a bit by passing my résumé along to Mrs. Ratner. "Oh, did I tell you what happened to Trevor, Barclay's creepy cousin?"

"Um, *no*." She grabs her bag off the kitchen table as we get ready to head downstairs for dinner. Barclay's reserved a booth in the back and is likely already waiting for us.

"He was fired last week. Canned and thrown out on his ass. He didn't even get a severance package."

"Let me guess," she pushes the down button for the elevator, "he was inappropriate with a woman at work?"

"Bingo!" I sound like I just called the winning number. "The company couldn't overlook his family connections after he was caught pressuring subordinates for sex, so the board told him to find the door."

"He's disgusting. I like sex, as you know, but can't stand men who prey upon women or pay for it. Gross." She shivers at the thought. "They need to earn it by treating us like ladies."

"True," I say. "Even your one-night stands need to take you out on a date."

We both laugh and enter the elevator to descend to the lobby. I pray dinner goes well for everyone, but mostly for my sweet man.

46

I throw back my bourbon and set the glass down on the bar. I've allowed myself one strong drink before dinner to calm my nerves. Hell, I don't think I've felt this worked up about meeting a girl's family since ... well, ever.

Miles has every right to "put me through the ringer," as Tessa calls it. I would feel the same way if I were in his shoes. But I'm not. I'm the one who has to prove himself worthy of Tessa, and I wonder if it's even possible.

I take a seat at the table I've chosen for us. It's to the side and back, leaving us more secluded from the hustle and bustle. There's a guy about my height with blond hair who just sat down at the bar and immediately strikes up a conversation with Michael, the bartender.

He fits Tessa's description of Miles and scribbles something on a small spiral pad. The kind you can fit into a pants pocket. It reminds me of a scene from Law and Order, and I know it's *him*—the man I have to impress.

I wipe my hands over my black wool pants as Jeffrey, our best server, comes up to the table.

"Good evening, Mr. Hammond. How are you this evening?"

I refrain from telling him my nerves are on edge and everything I hold dear is on the line if I fuck this dinner up.

"Hanging in there." I offer him a small smile.

"Would you like anything before the rest of your party joins you?"

"Bring me the bottle of Dom Perignon, two-thousand. But only open it once I give you the go-ahead. Thank you, Jeffrey."

When I look toward the front of the restaurant, Tessa walks in with a pretty brunette by her side. I assume it's Maggie, since the girl looks to be about Tessa's age. They make a beeline toward the blond guy at the bar, confirming he is Miles.

When the three of them start their way to my table, Miles and I lock gazes. A flash of recognition and surprise appears in his eyes. He knows who I am and turns to Tessa with a tightened jaw. The smile he was wearing has transformed into something close to a sneer. He says something to Tessa, and worry spreads over her face.

I stand up to greet them, but Miles' demeanor tells me this might not be the friendliest hello. My sweet girl looks about ready to cry and I fight taking her into my arms. Instead, I decide to try to save the dinner.

"Hello." I reach my hand out to Miles like it's a peace pipe. "Barclay Hammond."

"Miles Holly," he says, shaking my hand with a grip so tight it hurts. *Point made, good sir.*

"Miles, behave," Tessa whispers under her breath. "Barclay, this is Maggie, my bestie."

Maggie's jaw is somewhere in the Southern Hemisphere, and I have to smile. "Hi … um, wow!" she mutters.

"Great to finally meet you, Maggie." I reach to shake her hand, but she's frozen in place.

"You're … uh, so much better looking in person. I mean, you're super hot in all the internet photos. But wow. " She fumbles with her words, and Tessa laughs. Even Miles' frown has slipped into a straight line:

"Maggie, don't you have to run out and get something from the store?" Tessa looks like she has a nervous tick in her eye.

"Oh, yeah," she says, hitting her forehead. "I forgot. Hope to see you soon, Barclay. You wouldn't happen to have any hidden brothers or friends I could meet?"

"Bye, Maggie," Tessa says in a motherly tone, gently placing a hand on Maggie's back to move her along.

"Man, Tessa, you're one lucky bitch," Maggie whispers loud enough for me to hear.

"Imagine driving with her for two days." Miles rolls his eyes, and a side of his mouth tips up.

"She seems lively." I chuckle, and he nods. It's our first breakthrough, and I'll take anything at this point.

After Maggie leaves, Tessa sits in the chair next to me, and her brother takes one on the other side of the table, directly across from me. I'm not sure how we're going to stuff our long legs under the table, but it's clear he wants to access me, face to face.

I decided to be less formal tonight and dumped the monkey suit and tie, choosing to wear a fitted black V-neck T-shirt and dark jeans. Miles has on identical clothes. Aside from our opposite hair colors, we resemble six-foot-three bookends.

"I'm sorry for the tension, but I ambushed Miles," Tessa confesses, and Miles crosses his arms over his chest. "He didn't know you'd be here, eating with us."

"I hate surprises," he huffs.

Jeffrey's waiting a few feet from the table with the bottle of champagne. Figuring this is as good a time as any, I nod my head at him. He opens the bottle and has me try the first taste, then pours three glasses of bubbly.

I lift my glass. Tessa and Miles follow. "Cheers." We tap our glasses and sip on the liquid. Miles raises his brow in a sign of approval.

"Not bad," he says.

I want to tell him the bottle costs over five hundred dollars, so *not bad* isn't what I was aiming for, but I keep my cool and smile along.

"I hope you don't mind, but the chef is preparing something special for us," I tell them. "Filet mignon, corn crème brûlée, and asparagus."

"Sounds delicious," Tessa says. "Right, Miles?"

"Actually, it does." He rubs his toned stomach. "I've been eating fast food for two days on the road up here."

"I'm going to leave you boys alone to talk for a few minutes," Tessa says, getting up from the table, and I want to pull her back down into her seat. Her abandoning me wasn't in our plans. "I'll go chat with Michael at the bar." She grabs her flute and is off.

Miles stares at me, and I stare right back. Finally, he laughs, and I wonder what he's found so funny.

"You're nothing like I thought you'd be," Miles says, and I wait to hear if that's good or bad. "I've been walking around this hotel all afternoon, looking for one person to rat you out as a rich playboy. Funny thing is, they all seem to genuinely like you."

"That's good to hear." I exhale and lower my shoulders.

"They tell me the turnover rate is low. The pay rivals high-end hotels, and the benefits are unbeatable in the service industry."

"It's true. Just like you, I'm trying to follow in my father's footsteps, both here and at Hammond Press. Keep his legacy alive."

"Well, there you go and make me like you, too," Miles genuinely smiles at me for the first time. He eyes me for a minute, but I know he has something else to say. "I want to tell you a story, okay?"

"I'm game," I answer, having no clue what to expect.

"When I was seven years old, my mother brought Tessa home from the hospital. I'd never seen anything so small in my life. I was a big kid for my age, I bet you can understand." I nod, knowing how it was to always be the tallest in my class. "She was this delicate little bundle with blonde ringlets all dressed in pink. I knew she was special and made a vow beside her crib to be the best big brother on God's green earth."

"You've done a great job," I say, encouraging Miles. "And it's funny. I have a similar story."

"What do you mean?"

"In May, I sat in this very restaurant and noticed a beautiful young woman dressed in pink, blonde hair curled around her shoulders. I just couldn't look away from her if I tried. It took me a while to understand my feelings for her—believe our age difference was acceptable." Miles leans closer into the table, while Tessa beams at us from the bar. "But I can promise you this, Miles. I will never break her heart, though she has the power to destroy mine."

"I'll be damned," Miles says, laughing. "You really do love her, don't you?"

"With all my heart."

Miles nods at me, and it looks as if I've won over one of

the Holly men. Now, it's time to take a trip to Alabama and meet the rest of her family. I understand Southern fathers appreciate a man asking for his daughter's hand in person.

47

Barclay

One year later …

I have one more report left to go over before I can clock out for the night. Tessa said she was cooking up something special and would keep it warm for me. Her voice sounded seductive, like she had a hidden meaning behind her words.

Truth is, I can't keep her out of my pants. She wants sex more than a seventeen-year-old boy, but I can live with that … about twice a day.

As I finish the last page of the report, there's a knock at my office door. I glance at the clock, figuring Mrs. Mackenzie decided to stay late.

"Come in," I say without looking up from my computer. I need to get this work done so I can head home to my beautiful fiancée.

"Special delivery, Mr. Hammond," says a familiar voice—not belonging to my assistant.

One peek over my computer screen reveals a blonde goddess in a dangerously short trench coat. She holds a box in her hands. I lick my lips as she locks the door behind her.

"I don't remember ordering anything." I push back in my chair, crossing my arms over my chest.

"Well, you asked me to bring you a cherry tart." She holds up the bakery box, and I can't hide my amusement.

"I hope it's still warm." I give her a crooked smile, playing along.

"Very. Want to feel for yourself?" She saunters toward me, setting the box on a table.

She unbuckles her coat belt, and then starts to unbutton it, from top to bottom, torturing me in the process.

When she finishes with the last button, she walks to me, and the coat parts, revealing her beautiful, bare skin.

Her mouthwatering curves flow from full, firm breasts to soft, round hips. My fingers twitch from memory, needing to touch her now. I start to get up from my chair, but she raises her hand.

"Stay where you are, Mr. Hammond." The coat falls to the floor, leaving her bare except for her black stilettos.

God, I'm a lucky man.

She comes around the desk and kneels in front of me, rubbing her hands over my thighs. My dick presses against my suit pants, begging to be turned loose.

Unable to keep my hands to myself, I brush my fingers across the smooth skin of her cheeks, neck, and shoulder. She's so soft to the touch.

"Does the Hammaconda want to come out to play?" she asks coyly, using her nickname for my cock.

Jesus, what happened to the sweet virgin I met a year ago? I pray she never returns. I prefer this twisted version of her better.

"He's always ready for you, baby."

After easing my zipper down, she spreads the edges open, pulls my underwear down, and out he pops.

Giving my dick a name even has me referring to him in the third person, but he's happy, and so is she. That's all that matters.

Her mouth forms a big O, and she looks up with raised brows, like she's never seen a cock before. The minx might've missed her calling on Broadway.

"You're so large, Mr. Hammond. I've never seen anyone bigger."

When she bends forward, one of her hands encloses around me, pumping and giving me some relief. Then her tongue licks over me, and I lose my flipping mind as she takes me in her hot mouth. Suck, twirl, suck, twirl—over and over again.

She's perfected the art of giving head and knows what she's doing to me as I catch the twinkle in her eye.

After a few minutes, my release starts to build, but I haven't touched my favorite parts of her yet.

"Stop, babe." I place my hand under her chin. "I'd like to properly tip you for the special delivery." She nods, wiping her mesmerizingly pouty lips. *God, why did I stop her from sucking me off?*

Picking her up, I place her glorious ass on the edge of my desk and swipe everything to the sides, spilling items onto the floor. We're unleashed and wanton in our pursuit of pleasure.

"Lie back," I command.

She eases herself down onto the desk, golden hair cascading over the shiny mahogany wood. Breasts soft with blush pink nipples. Her legs dangle over the edge, and I part them, bringing the real prize into view.

I push my pants down farther, freeing my dick completely, and line myself up at her entrance. Before I take her, I rub over her already-wet sex, making sure she's ready.

"Come on, Barclay," she begs, greedily.

I cradle both her legs in the crook of my arms, spreading her even wider while holding her still. I don't want her falling off the desk.

With one thrust forward, I enter her.

"Oh, yes," I hiss.

"Harder, please. Harder." She always wants more.

"Touch yourself, sweet girl."

It's so hot watching her pleasure herself while I move in and out of her tight pussy. We're both edging closer, our bodies in sync and tightening, and finally, she lets go, mumbling in her special orgasm speak. Her muscles pulse around me, spurring my release.

I fall to the desk on my elbows, a panting, sweaty, satisfied man.

"Thanks for the special delivery, Tessa. What's the occasion?" I ask, as if she needs one. We've never fucked in my office before, not that I haven't wanted to.

"Look inside the box, please." She points over at the table.

I right my pants and walk to the box, picking it up and opening it.

"Surprise?" she says in a timid voice.

There's a small round cake with a pacifier sitting on top, like the one Beatrice used.

"What does this mean?" I ask, my eyes searching her face. "You're pregnant?"

"Yes. Are you okay with that? I mean, we've talked about kids in the future tense, and the wedding is in two weeks." I calm her worries with the happiest smile I can muster.

"Holy shit, I'm going to be a father." Overjoyed, I gently spin her around in my arms. "And yours is going to kill me."

"He'll get over it, especially if we name a boy after him, or a girl Holly."

"There are enough Barclay Hammonds in the world anyway."

I fall to my knees, placing my hands on her hips. Leaning

forward, I kiss her flat stomach, knowing our child is growing inside her. Talk about blowing my mind.

I have a sexy as fuck soon-to-be wife with a baby on the way. Plus, it doesn't hurt that she's a sex fiend. Hell, I'm one blessed man.

The End!

Made in the USA
Middletown, DE
08 August 2018